# SPANK ME

## A collection of twenty erotic stories

## Edited by Cathryn Cooper

Published by Accent Press Ltd – 2007
ISBN 1905170939 / 9781905170937

Printed and bound in the UK by
Creative Design and Print


Cover Design by
Red Dot Design

# Also available from Xcite Books:

**www.xcitebooks.com**

# Contents

# Master, Come For Me Again
## by Kitti Bernetti

My writing tasks are complete. Exhausted, I sit alone by the guttering candle and strain to hear his hard, familiar footstep on the paving below. I press a hand on the wine-coloured velvet bodice at my breast. It stills my constant heart, which thunders at the thought of Sir Hunter Tremayne.

So would yours, dear reader, had you been lucky enough to feel the kiss of his whip on your naked quivering skin. Please God let him ride his steed quickly to be at my side. I cannot resist agitating the curtain and peering down to the dark sodden earth below, willing, willing him to arrive. My ears strain for sound of approaching hooves, all they hear is rain drops spattering at the casement like pebbles. The clock ticks the minutes by interminably. It is bitter cold without him.

My quill pen agitates in its holder from the gale forcing its way in at the casement window. Sir Hunter will be with me soon. Very soon.

To pass the time, and keep me from pacing the room again, I take up the two documents on the desk and read the words on which I have been engaged. The first is my Last Will and Testament, completed an hour ago and signed by the cook, the housekeeper and the butler, now dismissed and in their beds. My three faithful witnesses.

*'I, Elizabeth Langdale, of Hampshire, England, being of sound and disposing mind and not being actuated by any duress, menace, fraud, mistake, or undue influence, do declare this to be my last Will, and that bequests detailed below be carried out in accordance with my wishes this day, the 15th December 18—'*

But, constant reader, you will be more interested in the second document I have written. It tells of my first meeting with Sir Hunter, of the things he taught me and the reasons for the strange bequest in my will. I am a woman of fortune and many would squabble over my leaving my considerable wealth to Frederick March, a mere servant, unrelated to me, if I did not explain the reasons for this curious bequest.

Come. Walk with me as I move aside the folds of my skirts and sit by the fire's fevered glow to remember. Read, read on…

'My tale starts the first day Sir Hunter had cause to speak to me. A poor child of fifteen, I had only briefly glimpsed the Master in the parish church of a Sunday. Head bowed in my distant pew, I would steal a glance at Sir Hunter's haughty figure, six feet of him, striding to take communion. I took pleasure in that arrogant bearing, the aristocratic nose down which he peered at those of us who were truly beneath him. Nothing would have induced me to approach the great man. What business would I, the daughter of a dairy maid, now a milkmaid myself, have had with such a pillar of our community? Our paths would only cross on these weekly occasions and I knew he never deigned to look at the likes of me.

However, I must correct myself. There was one isolated incident during which I witnessed a flicker of interest from Sir Hunter in my lowly self. It was a fine summer day, the sweltering heat taking all by surprise. I had swooned in church as if I would faint. The sermon droned interminably long, the heat seeped in unrelieved and the air hung sickly with the scent of drooping lilies in vases at the altar. Too timid to leave mid-service, I sought to relieve my distress by loosening the ties of my dress. My hand crept up to the sweat-glowed skin at my collarbone and down to the laces at my breast. Hoping no one was observing a mere farm girl, I took the laces and loosened each one. My eyes drooped at the relief afforded me and I fear I nodded off to sleep. Awaking, startled, I found the organ playing and the congregation rising at the end of the service. I confess I leapt to my feet, not quite knowing where I was. In so doing, the front of my loosened bodice fell away to reveal pert breasts and the small cherry brown of an escaped nipple. A small rivulet of sweat collected between the full globes and trickled onto the cotton of my chemise. Anguished at the realisation of my near undress, I grasped the cotton and self-consciously grasped it to my bosom. But not before I felt eyes upon me and looked up to find Sir Hunter's hungry gaze ravishing me. Something in that glance struck a chord within me. His look was stern with a sliver of harshness which prickled my belly. It reminded me of the look in a swordsman's eye just before he dispatches his prey. An appreciative quirk of his brow told me Sir Hunter had not only witnessed my distress but that he delighted in it. One word issued from his lips, 'slut'. A suffusion of pink overflowed my neck. Fearing I would faint, I grasped my little basket, gathered my shawl tightly to me despite the oppressive heat and escaped like a vixen with the devil at her heels.

Even with that moment of connection, and being under the same church roof many times after, Sir Hunter never rewarded me again with eye contact. I was as ignored and insignificant to him now as ever. I'm ashamed that I prayed (may the sweet Lord forgive me), alone in my bed, that circumstances were different. On occasions thoughts of him so invaded my head that my hands slid down under the hem of my nightshirt. Driving my fingers into my fevered body, I imagined with longing what it would be like to be explored by Sir Hunter's manicured fingers. But fevered dreams aside, we were stations apart in life. Gradually I accepted that his azure gaze would never alight upon a poor besotted milkmaid again.

Not until that is, the day three years later, in a grimy street in London town when I was astounded to find it was Sir Hunter's face which greeted me when I knocked at a strange door. But I move on too swiftly, dear reader, and risk leaving you behind. Let me explain. At the age of seventeen, happily living in the village and existing on glimpses of Sir Hunter for my amusement, I was shocked on returning to our cottage one day to find that my poor dear mother had passed away. Her passing was unexpected. Always a red-cheeked robust female, no one imagined that she could fall so completely to the consumption. Like a sturdy beech tree felled by the woodcutter's axe, one minute she was with us and the next, she lay in her coffin under the cold unforgiving ground, her sweet body giving way to corruption and the worms' attentions.

My grief was boundless. But it was compounded by the shocking realisation that I was now alone and stared that unforgiving curse, poverty, in the face. The kindly farmer who had employed us and who had supplied our meagre living accommodation succumbed to the coughing sickness the month after my mother. The new owner, a harsh man and a stranger in town, licked his fingers when he met me, lifted his chin and said, 'Now you're a right saucy creature and no mistake. Wouldn't I like to have your virgin lips to moisten my hardness?'

One night, alone asleep in my bed, I heard him enter the cottage he now owned. Whisky staling his breath, he wrenched off the bedclothes, gripped my neck and fondled me with his calloused hands. As he began to unbutton his britches, I panicked, kicked the drunken sot away and raced

4

out with only a dress, shawl and some pennies. With the little I had, I walked from village to village. But I was young, and growing painfully thin. At all the hiring markets, it was the voluptuous maidens or the clodhoppers with physiques of youths who were chosen for work. I was the girl left standing at the end of the day. I was the one who had been prodded and commented on and left with no employer willing to take a chance on me.

Like so many innocents before me, I made my way to London town to try my luck on its rat-infested pavements. Oh, those days of misery. Bent like an old crone, clutching a dirt-spattered shawl, I trudged through storms, my wooden pattens barely keeping my skirts above the mud. Sleeping under hedges, foraging for food, I existed on crab apples sour enough to turn milk.

When I finally reached the city it was alien to me, peopled as it was with rushing individuals clawing their living from the rancid alleyways. My last pennies, carefully preserved, I spent on a meagre room in a boarding house above a public house where I was able to wash my shattered body and clean my clothes. My only bit of luck in all those dark days was meeting a girl within lodgings near Fleet Street who had a country accent and was only a year or two older than myself. Perhaps recognising in my plight something of her own past, dear Martha possessed the looks and kind hands of an angel. She allowed me to share her accommodation and fed me for a fraction of the cost of a room of my own. Lighting a fire in the cosy attic room at the top of the house, and helping me dry my clothes she asked, 'And do you have any prospect of work here in London?'

'No,' I replied, 'but I have heard that anyone can find work here.'

'Hah, don't believe it. The streets are more paved with cabbage leaves than with gold. And sadly there's no call for dairymaids in these parts. Nevertheless, there is a gentleman who provides employment for young maidens like yourself. He is only in town sometimes, having a vast estate in the country so they say. But, he is here at present. I know because I was working for him myself only the other day.' At this point, she cupped my chin in her hands and stroking, fixed me with her gaze. 'You scrub up well dear little Lizzie. In fact I would say your rosebud skin and kitten-eyes would be most prized by this particular gentleman.'

'If this gentleman could help me I would do anything for him. Work hard on my knees, scrubbing floors and serving his every whim,' I told her. I guessed that industrious servants were hard to come by in London, but I would see him proud if he could rescue me from my plight. As Martha brushed my damp hair, petting it till it shone, I began to feel a spark of hope.

Martha continued, running her hands lovingly through my hair to dry it, 'He is very rich and only likes the finest of things. Girls queue up to be under his protection. But he is also very choosy. Not for him will any wench do.' She wound my waist-length hair around rags as she spoke. 'When I have set your hair, we will look in my cupboard and you can try on one of my old dresses. When I first came here I was as tiny as you. I have fattened up nicely since then but I am sure we can find you something better than that old grey woollen thing.'

Rifling in her bedroom cupboard Martha pulled out the most delectable midnight blue silk gown. 'Why, this is a rich woman's gown,' I cried, 'how did you come by it?'

Martha smiled. 'Oh there is money to be made in this town if you know how. And the gentleman I was speaking of will show you how, little Lizzie, as long as you let him, and do every thing he asks like a good girl.'

She helped me step into the gown and I stood as resplendent as a fine lady. Curves I had not before witnessed appeared under the tightness of the laced bodice and the full skirt. Down the neckline was sewn black lace and tiny black beads which twinkled in the candlelight. A neckline much lower than I was used to exposed the swell of my bosom but Martha only laughed at my concerns and told me the rich gentleman would have no qualms about that.

That night we lay together in her little bed. I was so grateful for all her help and for the way she held me close in her arms, 'to warm us,' so she said. She rubbed my back and my neck, 'to ease the aches and pains', and kissed me softly on the neck whispering in my ear that all would be well. I had never been caressed like that and it caused a strange moistening between my legs which embarrassed me.

My head spun when her hand moved to my chest. She giggled girlishly as she cupped my breasts, and exclaimed at how neat they were. Like little Bath buns fresh out of the oven she said, they needed tasting. I was a little shocked when she moved her lips down to my breasts and kissed them. I felt suddenly surprisingly warm and had to lift my nightshirt to cool me down.

Helpfully, Martha pushed it above my arms and over my head. It felt somewhat strange to be naked but perfectly safe with someone as kind and pretty as Martha. I felt she was getting a little warm too, I heard her breath quicken as she now feasted hungrily on my nipples, which had grown hard in a way I had never experienced before, except when I had washed myself in the depths of winter before going out to the cows.

Everything was so strange and different in this curious city; none more so than this crazy night. When Martha took her nightshirt off too, I was amazed at the size and volume of her breasts, heavy in the glowing light of the fire. Something deep in my stomach lurched and I found difficulty in breathing. I had never seen another human being unclothed before but supposed that as she was a girl and not a man there could be no harm in it. Martha lifted my trembling hand to touch her magnificent breasts. They were soft and full, like the cows' udders. Instinctively I pulled at her nipple like I did when I gently milked the cows and saw Martha's green eyes sparkle with desire.

It was so warm and comforting to see our bodies naked and bathed in fire flame. I lay back on the bed and felt Martha gently lift herself on top of me. Her little furry bush tickled the inside of my spread thigh. Driven by a burning passion I took her huge breast into my eager mouth and suckled. I felt a small sound like a purr come from my throat and felt my fingernails like little cat claws fasten into the bedclothes, as Martha emitted little moans herself. Without understanding why, I moved my legs apart, probably to cool my burning skin. At this, Martha moved slowly down, planting kisses over my flat belly, licking my belly button, down over my hipbones and down further still to my thighs. I felt her long silken hair fall against my cunny.

Then, dear reader, the most unbelievable sensation occurred as Martha pressed her warm wet mouth insistently between my thighs. I looked down in the firelight to see her tongue come out and gently lick me down there, her arse proudly sticking up as she knelt. The sensation was heavenly. I didn't think it could get any better until she madly quickened. I squirmed to get free not knowing what was happening to me. She held me fast with one hand, moaning while her other hand played in her moist bush. She increased her pace sending palpitations through my opening which convulsed my body in one arching spasm until I cried out to the moon. As I collapsed in a heap, I watched Martha laying back pleasuring herself alone to a shuddering completion.

After a superb night's sleep, Martha took out the cotton rags, tossing my black hair into bouncing curls. She announced that I should get dressed quickly and we would

8

both go to see the rich gentleman. She held my hand as we made our way down the labyrinthine streets. Finally at a small doorway, she kissed me and told me to knock and that the fine gentleman would be pleased to see us. Imagine my amazement when the door opened and there stood Sir Hunter Tremayne. I blushed hotly as his eyes ran slowly up my body, thinking he might turn me away. But he beckoned us both in, sat me down in the parlour room and, putting his arm around Martha, whispered with her in the hall. When he returned, Sir Hunter had a serious look on his face.

'Well, well. Little Lizzie Langdale. What a treat this is going to be. I am in need of your services. Come. We will start straight away.'

I held my head demurely in the presence of the great man, and Martha and I followed, into what appeared to be a large bedroom, suitable for a man of substance. I supposed that this was where I was to do cleaning or mending or some such. Sir Hunter sat in a chaise longue with his feet up and told Martha to take off my cape. 'She is pretty is she not?' He asked.

'Yes,' replied Martha. 'Very.'

Then his tone became harsh as he sat up and eyed me with a cruelty I had only seen a glimpse of once before. 'But, she is naughty too, is she not?'

'I believe she is, sir,' answered Martha. 'Very.'

He then got up and took a step towards me. 'Naughty girls should be punished should they not?' Terrified, I looked at Martha.

'Of course, sir,' answered Martha hungrily.

I stood transfixed at the sight of Sir Hunter's long limbs as he came towards me, not understanding any of this, unable to move. But, I was aware of my heart beating strongly and of a delicious hunger between my legs. Scared but anticipating at the same time, I smelt Sir Hunter as he approached. Leather and cigar smoke seemed to mingle on his breath, he was now so close. 'Bad girls deserve a

9

spanking,' he said gently in my ear, sending torrents of anticipation shooting through me. 'Get on your knees, girl.'

Not having it in my power to resist, I knelt down. Roughly he pushed me forward so I was on all fours. 'Martha,' he demanded, 'lift the little bitch's skirts'. Martha pulled up my dress, exposing my naked buttocks which tingled, so exquisite was the feeling of their exposure to this powerful man. In this state of subjugation, I watched as he went to the wall and took off it a horse whip, and a length of golden chord. My eyes pleaded with him as he stared me full in the face, then brutally tied each wrist to opposite chair legs and picked up the whip.

'Naughty, naughty, dirty little bitch.' His voice was gravelly as he played the whip over my exposed cheeks. The tender stroking across my white skin was delightful and terrifying. Then, the last thing I saw as he pulled back his arm and bought the switch cracking down on my buttocks was Martha's kindly smile, heavy with desire. The pain was exquisite, executed so elegantly by Sir Hunter, with such precision. Not only were my buttocks smarting, but the most intense sensation was the pleasure that the whipping had promoted in my quim. Sir Hunter brought the whip down again and I felt a swelling develop as I heard myself say weakly, 'please, no,' when what I really meant was 'please, yes.'

One last crack of the whip drove me wetly to shuddering orgasm and brought a sardonic smile to Sir Hunter's face. 'Now,' he said, 'for the ultimate punishment.' As I looked behind me, still on all fours, he unbuttoned his breeches and brought forth a huge specimen of manhood, erect as a sapling. On seeing it, Martha immediately sighed, dropped to the floor and took it in her mouth. I waited, watching her lapping like a little dog. Sir Hunter guided her, his hand at the back of her head, all the while looking me hard in the eyes. Then, he boomed. 'Enough,' wrenched his member out of her mouth and, stood behind me. Smiling, he parted

10

my thighs and rubbed his throbbing member over my buttocks. The power of it made me reach out and clutch his hugeness in my hand. Wet and hard, I marvelled at its strength. For a minute, Sir Hunter delighted in my hold, as I kneaded and played. Silently I begged for completion; when suddenly he lost patience. Brushing my hand angrily away, he roughly pulled apart my thighs, and forced his wet length into my widely splayed quim. In and out he drove while I cried out for mercy. In a matter of moments, he drew himself out and spattered his relief over the roundness of my buttocks, the warm seed dripping down my thighs. Martha licked her lips and smiled, knowing it was her turn to finish me off. The moment was too delicious, as her expert fingers drove round and round against my dripping sex. Martha, bless her, brought me shuddering helpless again to completion as she kissed me on the lips.'

Many times over the years to come I submitted to more delightful four-legged humiliation, always in the presence of the eager Martha. It took me some time to realise that Martha's desire was not for Sir Hunter but for me. They both took me to their separate beds and taught me all they knew. Martha loved me until the day she died last year, with the same devotion that I saved for Sir Hunter, my mentor and my master. As we two girls became women and reached maturity, and Sir Hunter grew slower, he installed us both in his country home for his endless pleasure. Under his expert education and care, I grew plump and voluptuous, delighting him with my curves, until now. As I write this, I am in my sixty-fifth year. I know I am going to die for I have this afternoon completed my will and had it witnessed by my servants. My final act has been to drink a phial of poison. Sir Hunter died last week at the venerable age of ninety-five, and the only place I wish to be is with him. I wait for his ghost to ride up on his horse and place my spirit form on its back so that we can ride away to meet up again with my dear old friend Martha.

11

There, you have my story as promised.

And the bequest? Well, that is to Frederick March, beloved bastard son of Martha March and Sir Hunter Tremayne. Somehow my own childlessness has not been so painful with little Frederick around, the offspring of the two most important people in my life. May he enjoy on earth the money which is no longer of any use to me. Ah, I feel life ebbing away from my body. I am done. I hear hooves clattering on the ground below. Please forgive me, I must depart. Sir Hunter is ready to take me away, to the other world, to be with him, my beloved master, and to welcome eternity and endless youth locked in his strong arms.

# Schooling James
## by Bryn Allen

She wanted to hit him. There was defeat written in the way James slouched over her battered kitchen table, written in the angry tension in his shoulders and the way his bright green eyes avoided hers. He'd given up, and Alice could think of jack shit that she could do to change his mind.

Leaning back, she blew out a frustrated breath. Between them were her tools, books, pencils, paper, calculator. Tonight, her third meeting with James, was to have been the grand battle, the fight that would have finally wrung some sign of surrender from her student and make him submit. Submit to finally learning something about statistics, so that they could salvage this last chance at a diploma. Now, it looked like the battle was over before she could even begin. 'Shit.'

'Yeah, exactly.' James shoved his book away, sent it sliding across the scarred wood into her books and sending pencils tumbling from the table like lemmings. 'This stuff's all shit. Why don't we just go for a beer?'

'Damn it, James, I don't want a beer. I want that fucking money that your father promised me if I could get you to pass. Why are you so committed to failing this test?' Alice stomped out with one foot, stopping a pencil from escaping beneath her refrigerator. 'You're this close to passing and getting your father off your back.'

13

'You think?' James shook his head. 'Not fucking likely. That old bastard won't be done until I'm as unhappy as he is. I should have dropped out last year.' He stood up, eyes stormy and body tense in its black jeans and T-shirt. 'Sorry Alice, I know you could probably use that bonus, but it's not happening. Just take what the bastard gave you for all these lessons and we'll skip the rest. I can use the time for rehearsal.'

'Wait.' James's hand was already on the door, twisting the knob, but he stopped. 'One more chance. Next week, one more. I'll figure out some way to beat this stuff into your head. C'mon.' His eyes flicked over his shoulder to meet hers.

'It's a waste of time. Fuck it though. I'll give you one last crack at me.' There was a smile in his voice as he opened the door and stepped through into the night. 'You're cute when you're frustrated.'

'I thought you gave up tutoring.' Eve dropped the glasses to the table, sending beer sloshing dangerously close to the rims. 'Wasn't worth it.'

'It wasn't. Then this bastard upped the price.' Alice waited until the beer had settled before picking it up for a long swallow. 'Paid me as much to prep one kid for one test as I made off of doing five for a whole semester. And promised me triple if he passed.'

'Nice. Except the kid…'

'Won't. Hates school, hates his dad, hates the class. Doesn't hate me, but then we've had less than three hours together and he spent most of that staring at my tits.' Alice set down the beer. 'I thought it might work. He's not stupid. When he listened, he got this shit. But James doesn't want to listen; he'd rather be playing his bass.'

'Bass? James?' Eve cocked an eyebrow at her. 'James what?'

'James Miller.'

14

'James Miller? Plays for Bend and Deliver? Tall, dark hair, good-looking in that suspicious, mischievous sort of way that makes you think you'd be better off with out him, once you've had one last good fuck?'

'I'm not quite sure about that, but yeah, sounds like him. Know him?'

Eve snorted. 'I went with him for a couple of months two years ago. Don't you remember me talking about him?'

'No.'

'Thick-dick?'

'James is thick-dick?' Alice remembered her friend's stories. 'You said he was younger, but...'

'He was nineteen, and I wasn't thirty. Yet. Anyway, there you go.' Eve smirked at her over her glass.

'What?'

'That's how you motivate him.'

Alice frowned at her friend. 'What the hell are you suggesting?'

'You want him to listen, right? And you said he's been checking you out. So offer to fuck him if he passes. Ample motivation for a man.' Eve settled her glass down and gave Alice her most reasonable look. 'Look, he was a nice guy, which is fucking rare in a musician, and a fabulous fuck. I wasn't kidding when I called him thick-dick, and he knew how to use it. If Landon hadn't come back from New York, I wouldn't have let him get away. What a piss-poor decision that was.'

'I'm not a whore, Eve.'

'Course not. You wouldn't be broke if you were. It's just a more... traditional teaching method. You said he'd learn if you could get him to pay attention, and you've got a great attention-getter right there under your skirt.'

'Eve, I'm this close to pitching this beer in your face.' Alice tapped the glass warningly.

'Fine. I try to help.' Eve leaned back, eyes tragic. Then she grinned. 'Hey, if you don't want to reward him, you

15

could at least threaten him.' Alice rolled her eyes pointedly away, but Eve kept going. 'Didn't I tell you about his kink? Must've been too focused on the girth issue. James loved being spanked. Loved it. I ever wanted to get him ready, a couple of whacks on the backside and boom, at attention and raring to go.'

'And this information helps me how?'

'Well, if he doesn't listen to you, give his ass a good smack. That'll get him focused. Show him a little discipline from the headmistress, right?'

'Yeah. You're a great help, Eve. Wonderful advice. Screw him or smack his arse.' Not that the idea of cracking the lazy punk across the backside didn't have its appeal. Especially since it was such a nice backside. Alice shook off the idea and stood. 'Another round?'

'Of course. And hey,' Eve snagged her hand as Alice started to walk away, 'if you haven't figured out that you can deal with ninety-five percent of your problems with men with one of those two options, it's no wonder you aren't getting laid.'

Alice scrubbed the damp towel through her hair and stared at the clothes she had laid out on the bed. Dark skirt, long, buttoned neatly down the side. Black shirt, long-sleeved, collared, buttoned. Black hose that reached up to mid-thigh. Black bra and panties, lacy, see-through, sexy. And there it was, right there. This wasn't just some last desperate attempt to claim the money James's father had promised her for success. If it was, she could have worn her regular old cotton underwear. This was, at least partly, about sex.

'Hell,' she whispered, and dropped the towel. Ever since she'd talked with Eve the idea had been growing. It tried to hide itself in logic at first. This was the only way she had of getting through to him. He didn't need this degree, a rich kid, member of a band that was getting some interest on the local scene, maybe even beyond. Why not take a chance, see what happened? It might work, and she might get her bonus. It might work, and she might see those green eyes look at her with something other than irritation at being forced to do a hated task or the casual speculation of boredom. She might see them flicker with desire.

Alice reached out and picked up the panties and stepped into them. They were snug, silky smooth. Wearing them, she felt more naked. Almost a year without a boyfriend, without a lover, too caught up in her writing and jobs and stress. 'So what if it is about sex. I could fucking use some.' With a wry smile, she began to pull on the rest of her outfit and plot out the character she was going to play.

Standing in her tiny kitchen, Alice looked up at the grinning cat clock on the wall and tapped her fingers on her arm. James was ten minutes late, and if he didn't show soon she was going to lose all her nerve. In the night dark glass of the door, she could see herself, arms folded and face tense. The look was right at least, her rigid posture complementing the glasses she wore tonight and the tight bun that held her hair. The costume was good, the scene was set, and she'd been practicing her lines, but now the audience was absent. Alice frowned at her dark reflection and wondered if she should be relieved or disappointed when the dark glass vibrated with a hard knock.

'Come in,' she called, making her voice as hard and level as possible. James was dressed as usual, dark boots, faded jeans and a crumpled T-shirt tight enough to show off the lean strength of his chest and arms. He stopped at the door to stomp out the butt of a cigarette, then came in, looking her over curiously.

'You're late, Mr Miller,' she said in the same firm voice. It surprised her that she could keep it that way while butterflies swarmed through her stomach. Maybe she should have trained as an actress instead of a playwright. Apparently she had some talent, and in any case she'd be just as unemployed.

17

'Yeah, I know. Look, I'm just here…'

'Mr Miller, you're here to learn statistics. No more, no less.' Alice reached down and lightly slapped the cover of the textbook that sat alone on the table next to her. 'A task you have been shirking.'

'What's up, Alice?' He seemed more amused than anything else, clearly trying to figure out her new attitude, the sudden change from her usual chumminess.

'Ms Smith, Mr Miller. That is how you will address me. As for what is up, the answer is your time for lollygagging around. I've had quite enough of your attitude. It is time now, I believe, for stricter methods.'

'Really? Like what?' James leaned against the door, grinning at her, sensing some kind of game at hand. For some reason, that sly grin pushed the butterflies right out of Alice. This might have started as some sort of ploy on her part, a last half-assed attempt to provoke some interest from her student, but now her palm suddenly itched to wipe that smile from his face.

'Mr Miller, I recall that at the end of our second lesson, I assigned you twenty problems to complete. May I have them?'

'What?' He was still grinning, but his eyes were a little uncertain as she kept the steel in her voice.

'I take it that you have not completed them then. Any of them.' Alice shook her head. 'Mr Miller, I'm quite disappointed. Come to the table.' James arched an eyebrow at her, but she didn't blink. 'Come here, now.' Still staring at her, he slowly pulled himself off the wall and crossed to her. Looming over her, tall, broad-shouldered, she could smell the sharp scent of soap overlying the thin trace of his sweat. 'Now bend and take hold of the table edge, Mr Miller.'

'Why?' he asked her. His grin was gone, and his eyes had a wary mix of suspicion and anticipation.

'I'm afraid you've left me no choice, Mr Miller. My earlier benevolence has obviously failed. So now we shall try something more traditional, more strict. Bend over.' She made the words menacing, but had to fight to keep a nervous smile away. Then, amazingly, he did it. Turning from her, he leaned over and grasped the table edge. Alice stared at him, not quite believing it for a moment. This man, young, attractive, rough, bending at her command... her eyes went down to his ass, round and tight in his dark jeans, and a quiver ran through her. She owed Eve an apology.

'How many problems were you assigned?'

'Twenty, ma'am.'

*Ma'am.* Alice savoured the word, watched James' body tense as he waited in the silence. Time stretched as she let his anticipation build, before she continued. 'Twenty.' Drawing back her hand, she hesitated. *How hard?* Staring at his body, hard and strong, she decided quickly that it was unlikely she could hurt him with a bare hand slap on the backside. It was more likely he would barely feel it. Widening her stance a bit, she wound up and readied herself. 'You will count to twenty for me then.' Then she swung, whipping her hand about to catch him on the lower curve of his right cheek.

The sound was louder than she thought; a sharp crack that echoed in the tiny kitchen. The strike jarred her, made her palm hot, but James barely moved. 'One,' he whispered. Her palm might burn, but it was nothing now compared to the sudden fire between her legs.

'Count more loudly, James,' she ordered and swung again. Harder. This time he moved as her hand struck his other cheek, rocking slightly.

'Two,' he spoke, voice harsh. Ignoring the sting in her hand, Alice wound up again. 'Three...Four...Five...' Alternating from one side of his arse to the other, she struck harder with each slap as he called out the number. On the last five, he barely had time to call out the count, and his

19

'Twenty!' was more of a bellow than a number as she struck him for the last time.

Done, Alice stared at James leaning over the table panting and watched the trickles of sweat that ran down from his dark hair over the hard lines of his face. Breathing hard herself, Alice's whole body burned with exertion, lust, and a fierce possessiveness. She leaned forward and wrapped her fingers into the long strands of hair that flowed across his neck, turning his head to her. His eyes were bright with the same hunger she felt.

'Listen carefully to me, Mr Miller. I am your teacher. You will do as I say, do you understand? You will study, do your work, and pass this test. Understand?' His head moved against her hand in acknowledgment. 'Good.' Releasing him, she stepped away and wiped her palm across her breast, fighting for poise. She wanted... wanted... But not yet. Not tonight. She could stay in control.

But could he? The muscles in his jaw were bunched and twisted as if he were trying to swallow back his need. Alice straightened herself up, made herself iron. 'Twenty problems, Mr Miller. Go home and do them. Then bring them back here on Thursday.' His face was dark with frustration, and she could almost hear his body hum with tension. 'Show up without them, and I'm afraid I'll have to give up on you. No more lessons. Understand?'

'Yes, ma'am.' A rasping whisper.

'Thursday then.' Only after the sound of his car was gone did she let herself relax, sliding down the wall to rest on the cold tiles. Her palms stung, her arm ached, and between her legs a fire burned.

On Thursday, he showed up with his problems complete. Alice corrected them, savagely drawing a large red X through the wrong answers. Ten wrong. Adding ten more strokes for bad penmanship, that was twenty more strikes, again with her hand, but she made him pull his pants down this time. Each time she struck, she could see the red mark

20

of her palm on that lovely skin, and when she was done he was crimson. Twenty new problems, then, and she told him to come back on Sunday afternoon.

On Sunday, only six wrong. Alice congratulated him, before taking exception again to his writing, and his attitude. Twenty strikes. In the bright afternoon sun that streamed in through the windows, she made him pull down his pants and bend over her lap so that she could stripe him with the wooden ruler she had bought just for it. As he jerked from its sting, she could feel his cock pressing hard against her thighs. Eve had been right, he was thick, and as the ruler cracked Alice had felt herself growing wet, wondering how it would feel to take that thickness in. She could fill herself up with him, let him stretch her as she wrapped her legs around his waist... The thought made her lose track of her count, and she had to start again. James didn't argue.

Ignoring the damp spot he'd left on her skirt, she'd told him to come back on Tuesday. James had to remind her that that was when his test was. 'Well then. If you pass, I expect I will see you Wednesday to go over the test.' Alice had made her gaze cool and level as she said it, meeting his burning eyes. After he'd gone, she wondered what would happen if he failed, if he didn't show up. 'Little bugger better not take it that literally,' she growled to herself, rubbing her fingertips across her skirt front. The bonus had become a much less important issue for her.

Wednesday evening and Alice paced nervously through the house. As the night deepened, she wondered if she should call him, but slapped the impulse down. That wasn't how this worked. She was the teacher, and he would come to her. Still, when the back door finally rattled, she heaved a sigh of relief and had to work hard to keep from running to it.

'Let's see.' Alice held out her hand, frowning slightly at James, barely keeping the excitement she felt from leaking out. James was doing an excellent poker face behind his sulking schoolboy act, and she would live up to it. Finally, he jerked a folded sheet out of his back pocket and handed it to her.

Alice made a production of it, slowly unfolding the paper and staring silently at it through her glasses. 'Well, Mr Miller.' A hot stirring ran between her legs, making them wobbly, but she stayed straight. 'Adequate. You managed to pass. Well then.' She reached out her hand and held it in front of him. His act slipped a little as he stared at it in confusion, then reached out to take it. Alice gave him a firm handshake. 'Congratulations young man. You won't have to deal with me any more, will you? No more discipline from the old bat, right?' The look in his eyes had an edge of panic. 'You're lucky, really, considering how my palms itch just looking at that C. You would have had an A if you'd only applied yourself. Very lucky, Mr Miller.'

'I suppose…'

'Suppose what?' She stepped close to him, almost brushing against him, to stare up disapprovingly. 'Suppose you could have done better?'

His mouth stretched into that cocksure grin. 'You really think I could have satisfied you?'

'If you…' His lips crushed her words into her as he pressed them against hers. Lust washed through her, made her want to wrap her arms around him as his tongue brushed between her lips, but she pushed him away.

'How dare you, James.' The words were right, but the shaky eagerness of her voice wasn't in character. 'That was very, very bad. You're going to suffer for it.' Her hands reached out, grasped the buckle of his belt and yanked it free. He rocked a little then balanced himself as she slipped the thick leather strap from his belt loops. Wrapping it around her hand, she pointed to the table. 'Take your position, Mr Miller. And take off those clothes.'

He did as he was told, though he never lost his smile. His body was hard and lean, the skin dark with sun except for the pale band around his groin and over his arse. That smooth white skin pulled her eyes to it, the round swell of his buttocks ripe for punishment, the heavy, jutting thickness of his sex promising a sweet punishing pleasure of its own. When he leaned forward, she couldn't stop herself from reaching out and sweeping her hand down his back to his bottom. 'Bad boys get punished, James. Punished badly.'

The first stroke was light, barely tapping him. The leather belt was wide and flat, and she feared havoc if she swung too hard. Slowly though, her arm drew back, swinging the belt harder. The fourth stroke left a nice red line across both cheeks. By the seventh, both cheeks were flame red. On the eleventh, he groaned as he was struck, breath hissing through clenched teeth.

'Between one and ten more strikes, James. How many do you deserve?' Alice had spent some time reading up on this sort of thing on the internet, getting ideas.

'Ten more, Ms Smith. I was very bad.'

'Yes, you were. Now count.' The belt cracked, and Alice ever so carefully edged up its power with each stroke until the last one almost knocked him over. Breathing deep, she stared at the flaming skin of his backside. He'd have marks from this that would last awhile: her marks, and the thought inflamed her more. Lightly, she drew her fingers across the sensitive skin, watching him jerk. 'Maybe now you'll remember your manners, James.' Alice let her hand circle lazily, sending it around his hip to find the rigid heat of his cock. She tapped it lightly, and then circled her fingers around it, liking its weight in her hand. 'Though sometimes, James, I'll wonder if you'll ever learn.' Her lips brushed his ear as she whispered to him, and she gave his sex a gentle squeeze.

23

'Not today, ma'am. Not today.' He moved fast, and Alice barely had time to release him as he twisted towards her, catching hold of her and scooping her up to dump down on kitchen table. Alice sprawled backwards, palms slipping on the wood as he jerked at the skirt, popping buttons free and sending them skittering across the kitchen.

'You are being very bad now, James,' Alice hissed at him, shifting her hips to help him as he pulled the skirt open, exposing her up to the hips.

'I know. I can't wait to see what you do to me for this.' His fingers wrapped around the wet fabric of her panties and Alice felt a blaze of pleasure as they brushed across the lips of her sex. He jerked the silken barrier down her legs and off, then came forward again, his cock brushing her thighs as he pushed close.

'Wait,' warned Alice, barely able to say the word around the raging desire that demanded her to spread herself wide. Fingers did a clumsy dance as she fished in a shirt pocket for the slick square of plastic hidden there. 'You need a fucking rubber. What the hell do they teach you university boys?'

'Not enough about fucking.' He ripped open the plastic and stretched the condom over his cock. 'But don't worry, I've practiced.'

Alice felt him, the head of his cock pushing against the lips of her cunt, pressing them aside as it slipped forward. She was wet and ready, but still he had to push in slowly to let her body ease around him. 'Oh, very, very good Mr Miller,' she moaned.

'Just… just trying to please, Ms Smith,' he gasped back.

'Don't call me that. Call me ma'am.'

'Yes, ma'am.' Out, and then back in, faster when Alice raised her hips and wrapped her legs around him. Her heels brushed his abused bottom and he flinched, and sped up more. Alice laughed and pushed her calves down, rubbing across his backside, making him growl with pain and

24

pleasure, making him fuck her harder until she felt the pleasure build to a spiking climax that made her sprawl back on the table and gasp out a long release, only dimly aware that James was pressing hard into her, groaning his own climax as his cock jerked in her.

Later, he apologised about her skirt, and Alice smiled. He was nice, especially for a musician, like Eve had said. Alice told him they could settle that later, and when he left, she kept his belt.

# My Initiation
## by Eva Hore

My best friend Rita has met a new guy and can't stop talking about him. Said he was wild and uninhibited. Loved sex and role-playing. At first I thought she was exaggerating but after having met him I knew that all she said had to be true. His name was Marcus and the guy was fucking gorgeous. I must admit I am very envious.

I was also a bit put out with all the attention she was giving him. We've shared an apartment for nearly five years. Both of us are bi-sexual and we've always enjoyed each other's bodies as well as company. Now that she was always seeing Marcus she had no time for me.

Anyway, I was lying on my bed, and to be honest I was just thinking about Marcus, when Rita startled me at my door. I felt guilty, as though I'd actually done something with him and my face flushed scarlet.

'Staying in tonight are you?' I asked hopefully, noting she was only wearing skimpy underwear under her half-opened robe.

'No. I'll be leaving shortly,' she said.

'So what's up?'

'Well, I've got a proposition to put to you,' she said, a cheeky smile causing her luscious lips to quiver.

'What do you mean?' I asked.

'Well, you know how Marcus likes to experiment with

different scenarios and stuff?' she prompted.

'Yeah.'

'Well, I was just wondering… you know… if you're not doing anything tonight…' she stammered.

'Yeah,' my interest was definitely piqued.

'Well, we've been trying out this new game…and Marcus has a two way mirror in another room…and like he won't know you're there…he won't be able to see you or anything… and I was just wondering if you'd like to watch us…you know…having sex?'

'You're kidding?' I practically choked on the words

God, would I? Who wouldn't?

'You don't have to…it's just that since I've met him…well *we* haven't had much time together…I hardly ever see you now…and I don't know…I just thought you might be interested.'

'You mean, while the two of you are having sex, I'll be in a room on my own watching?' I asked, my pussy throbbing at the thought of it.

'Yeah,' she smiled. 'It'll be wild. He won't know you're there, but I will. It would really turn me on,' she said, coming closer to me, so close that I could feel her breath on my neck when she sat down on my bed beside me.

I hadn't had good sex for ages. Whenever we felt randy we'd just, you know, get each other off, better than masturbating on your own. Anyway it had been a while because she'd been so busy with Marcus. I wanted to say no, pretend I was going out, but when her hand stole its way up my thigh, the word no fell from my lips. I wanted to go and see what Marcus was really like, you know, buck naked and performing but something inside niggled at me.

'I don't think so,' I said. 'It would be too weird,' I gasped as her fingers gently pushed my thighs apart.

'No it wouldn't. You know you'd love to watch. How many times have we talked about it? It's everyone's fantasy,' she continued, her teeth now gently nipping the

28

flesh of my neck.

'Yeah I know. But fantasies are exactly that. Thoughts you keep in your head. This would be different. I don't think I could do it,' I said.

Her lips were brushing over the swell of my breast as she spoke, hardening my nipples.

'Sure you could,' she insisted. 'I could show you around his apartment and you could see all his kinky stuff that I've been telling you about. What do you say?' she asked, her fingers roaming inside the crotch of my panties.

'I think you should stay here tonight with me,' I said, grabbing her hand and holding it in between my thighs where I squeezed tightly.

She pushed me back down on the bed, dropping the robe off her shoulders before her hand slipped inside my panties. I grabbed her breasts freeing them from her bra. I opened my legs wider allowing her fingers to roam around my lips, while I squeezed her nipples between my fingers, knowing how much she liked it.

'Hmm, I'd say you really like that idea, judging by how wet your pussy is,' she laughed, beginning to finger me.

'I've missed you,' I said, kissing her mouth. 'I've missed you a lot.'

Her swaying breast fell into the palm of my hand as I groped for it, enjoying the heaviness, the weight of her flesh.

'Me too,' she whispered, 'it's been too long.'

Extracting her fingers she smeared my silky juices over my clit, rubbing, as only another woman knows how. I held her hand there, enjoying the sensation and then her mobile phone rang.

'Shit,' she said.

'Don't get it,' I begged, on the verge of coming.

'I have to. It might be Marcus,' she said, leaving me as she rushed from the room. I quickly pulled off my panties and threw them on the floor, pulling back the hood from my clit I rubbed frantically. I needed an orgasm desperately.

Coming back into my bedroom with the phone to her ear, she eyed me from the doorway. I knew how much Rita loved to watch me masturbating so I put on a show for her, one I wanted her to remember, rubbing myself, lifting up my arse, begging her to come back and finish her job.

She came closer to the bed, still talking on the phone and lowered herself to the floor on her knees between my legs. Her face was just inches away from my pussy. I watched her tongue snake out to lick me. My pussy ached for her.

With her fingers on her lips indicating to me to be quiet, I held back, falling onto the pillows, with my finger poised on my pulsating nub while she spoke.

'No, that's fine, honey,' she said. 'Sure, I'll be there in an hour…what…yeah, I'll hang on.'

She lay her head between my open thighs pushing the end of the phone inside my pussy, while her tongue licked crazily at my clit. I was so turned on. I arched upwards, moaning, but a quick smack on my thigh reminded me I was supposed to be quiet. Crushing my own breasts I stifled a scream as my first orgasm escaped me.

Rita was pushing the phone in and out of my pussy and I bucked into it, wanting her tongue in my pussy not the phone. I grabbed the pillow and covered my face, trying to muffle my moans, while coming again.

'Yeah, I'm still here,' she giggled, removing the phone and rising, looking down at my gaping pussy. 'Oh, I'd love that…yeah, sure…I'll have everything ready. I love you,' she said before disconnecting the call.

'You fucking horny little bitch,' she said, as she devoured me. 'I've missed your gorgeous pussy.'

I grabbed the back of her head with both hands pulling her into me as her teeth grazed my clit.

'Get your G-string off,' I demanded. 'Bring your pussy up here so I can give you a good tonguing.'

'I can't,' she mumbled.

'Just for a few minutes,' I begged.

She pulled back smiling. 'I have to go. Change of plans. Marcus is coming home early and he wants me to be ready when he gets home, so come on, cover that hot pussy and let's get going.'

'I can't,' I said.

'You sure?' she asked, her eyes fixed on my open thighs, her tongue licking her finger as she eyed my breasts before rubbing her saliva over the nipple and giving it a squeeze.

I was still in two minds about going. I really wanted to, wanted to go and watch but thinking about fantasies and acting upon them can sometimes be disastrous. I needed more time to make a decision.

I shook my head.

'You'll be sorry,' she said, picking up her bra and robe, before sauntering to the door.

She looked back over her shoulder at me, arching her eyebrow. Her naked back tapering down into her sexy arse tempted me, so I looked away, disappointed at having had our time cut and not wanting to change my mind.

As soon as she left, I lay there hugging myself, wishing I'd said yes. The thought of witnessing some live sex had certainly been something we'd talked about. What was the matter with me? Why had I said no?

Pulling on a robe I made my way into Rita's bedroom. I stood there in the middle of her room, imagining the two of them buck-naked on her bed. I visualised what they'd look like, how I'd join in, what they'd do to me.

I moved over to her bed, dropping the robe as I did and lay down on my back. Grabbing the duvet I pulled it between my legs, inhaling her scent, the faint lingering of her perfume reminding me of other times I'd spent in here with her.

I rose, carefully opening drawers, snooping around for something but not knowing what it was that I wanted. Underneath her bed I found a photo album. I flipped the pages over, shocked to see page after page of her tied up and being whipped. Red welts covered her body and there were some close-ups of her pussy, all swollen, glistening with her juices.

This side of Rita surprised me. We'd done a bit of experimenting ourselves but never actually spanked each other. We'd tied each other up for fun, had rough sex, but had never actually physically inflicted any pain on each other.

I lay back on her bed, holding the photo album close to my chest, imagining I was with her now, exploring Marcus's apartment before he came home, just like she'd said we could.

'Pretty cool, isn't it?' Rita would say after giving me a quick tour.

'Wow, check out the waterbed. It's huge,' I'd comment as I entered his bedroom.

'And so much fun, I can tell you. Listen, he'll be here soon, so I'll take you into his hidden room,' she'd say, pulling open mirrored wardrobe doors.

I'd be eager and happy to hide in there, in a cupboard that had a hidden panel where the clothes slid across to open to a walk-in room. There'd be an armchair in there and on the wall would be racks with dildos, whips, handcuffs and things I've never seen before. There'd even be a video camera; a camera where I could record the events as they unfolded and take home with me to watch when I was feeling frustrated.

'Just make yourself comfortable in the chair and when he comes home you'll be able to hear and see everything. Just be quiet, OK?' she'd whisper.

'Sure,' I'd say, watching her as she'd quickly open drawers to remove whatever she needed. I'd stay there while she slid the door back, closing me in, giving me no where else to go, ensuring I'd see it all.

I'd watch as she'd touch up her face, perfume her neck,

slather her lips with gloss before changing into a skirt and skimpy blouse and then she'd sit demurely on his bed to wait. I'd wonder what he would do if he discovered that I was hiding in his secret room.

I found myself holding my breath, my heart pounding as I continued to play out this fantasy in my mind.

I squirmed on the bed, luxuriating in my nakedness. I grabbed a pillow and hugged it to me. It was thick and soft. I pushed it down between my thighs, squeezing them together, enjoying the sensation of it as I thrust my pelvis into it.

I lay on my side, my hand stealing its way down to cup my pussy, but it wasn't enough so I stared up at the ceiling, imaging Marcus above me, looking down at me, admiring my body, tweaking a nipple before his mouth covered it and sucked it in between his hot lips.

I flipped through the album but all the photos were of Rita. I wanted a visual of Marcus, something to focus on, so I wiggled over to the side on my belly, my pussy creaming her duvet. I looked down under the bed and found a box. Inside the box were photos of Marcus, nude photos of him lying in every position imaginable, his thick cock lying like a salami on his open thigh. His cock was huge just like she'd told me.

Some of the photos were of Rita sucking his cock, close-ups of her mouth swallowing him, her lips stretched to accommodate its girth. Some photos have only his eyes and nose peeking over her hairy bush as his mouth must have been working its magic on her pussy.

I imagined him nuzzling between my thighs, licking and sucking while his strong hands groped for my breasts and squeezed hard. I held onto a photo in one hand while the other slipped between my folds, enjoying the wetness as I gently rubbed my clit, before dropping the photo to really give it a good working over.

I climaxed, seeing Marcus in my mind, his eyes boring

into mine, more handsome than his photos. I'd only seen him once before, when I was running late and they were walking to his car. Rita had introduced us quickly. There was something animalistic about him. I think it was the way he walked. He was confident with himself and his sexuality oozed out of every pore. He was tall with a great body. He'd been wearing a tight shirt, his torso magnificent, rippling with muscles that diminished down to a nice arse and strong legs.

I closed my eyes tight, imagining I was locked in the closet in his room. He'd enter and walk straight over to Rita.

'Hello Rita,' he'd say.

She'd say nothing. Just sit there, with her head bowed down as though she didn't even know that he was there.

'Rita, I said hello. Didn't you hear me?' he'd ask.

She'd looked up coyly, a slight smile on her pretty face.

'Well?' he'd ask.

She'd continue to stare at him, challenging him, while I'd be sitting quietly perched on the armchair observing all.

'It's rude you know, not to acknowledge someone when they speak to you. Did you know that?' he'd say.

Still she'd say nothing, eyeing him defiantly, as though daring him to be angry with her. He'd undo his tie and throw it on the dressing table taking a few steps towards her while rolling up his sleeves. With his feet slightly apart, he'd place his hands on his hips and continue to stare at her.

I could see it all vividly in my mind so I kept my eyes shut tighter and breathed in deeply, desperate not to lose the momentum.

'You're being a naughty girl,' he'd say, undoing his buttons to expose a hairy chest.

'I'm not!' she'd pout.

'Oh, so you've found your voice. You're being a very naughty girl, Rita. Come here so I can punish you. Come on,' he'd demand, sitting on his chair behind his desk.

34

She'd stay on the bed.

'Do you like being a bad girl?'

*I wanted to be a bad girl.*

'No.'

'Then why haven't you come over here like I asked?'

'Because,' she'd say, looking up at him through dark lashes.

'Come now!' he'd demand, his voice rising with authority.

She'd rise and walk slowly and seductively towards him.

His desk would be close to the mirror. The chair directly in front of where I would be sitting, as I poised on the edge, eager to see what would happen next. He'd push backwards and the chair would roll even further towards me. He'd swivel it out on an angle and pull her closer to him by the hips, between his outspread legs. Then he'd sit there with his arms crossed staring at her for a few moments.

'I don't know what I'm going to do with you,' he'd say.

She'd suck on a finger before pulling down her bottom lip. She looks sexy doing that and I'd wonder if she was thinking about me, as her eyes would sweep across the mirror.

'You've been a bad girl and now I have to punish you. I want you to bend over my knee,' he'd say.

Giggling, she'd do as he asked. Pulling up her skirt he'd run his hands over her panties and begin to spank her with light smacks. When she doesn't respond, he'll spank her harder.

'Oww,' she'll whimper.

'That's what happens when you're a naughty girl,' Marcus will chuckle.

'I'm not naughty,' she'd pout.

'You are. Now be quiet,' he'll say as he gives her a harder smack.

'You're hurting me,' she'll whine. 'Please stop. I promise I'll be good.'

Marcus will keep on slapping her, ignore her pleas.

'I said that's hurting,' she'll say more loudly.

'It's supposed to hurt, Rita, and don't raise your voice to me. You've been a naughty girl, and now that you have raised your voice I think I'll need to punish you some more,' he'll say.

I'll have a perfect view of her arse. I can feel my own pussy begin to throb, as I think about him slowly peeling down her panties. Her cheeks will be red and in this position I'll be able to just see her pussy lips glistening with her juices as she squirms over his lap.

He'll rub his palm over both cheeks, a finger slipping down her crack and she'll move her hands back to her panties, trying to pull them up, to cover herself. He'll smack them away. She'll try to get up, her legs opening wider as she does, but he'll hold her down.

'Oww!' she'll cry.

'You shouldn't have put your hands there. You know I don't like it when you disobey me. Now I'll have to spank you with the ruler.'

I allow my legs to fall open slipping a finger inside. Oh, nice and wet, very wet. I slap at my pussy, enjoying the sharp stings as they hit my pussy lips, my clit and the soft flesh inside my thigh. I push my fingers inside me, squeezing my thighs shut as I try to conjure up more of this fantasy.

With Rita still balanced on his knee he'll withdraw a ruler from one of the drawers. It will give me the opportunity to admire his handsome face. Chiselled features with a short crew cut. He looks like a model with his tanned skin and brilliant blue eyes. I'll push my body up close to the glass, pretending it's not there, that I'm pushing myself into him. He'll quickly glance over at the mirror and I'll pull back startled as though he's stared straight through me.

*I'll wonder if Rita has somehow told him that I'm watching from behind the mirror.*

36

Rita's arse will become even redder as he hits her with the ruler. He'll expertly slip her panties down to her ankles, slide them off one leg to leave them dangling on the other. With his free hand he'll push her legs apart, give himself, and me, a nice view of her pussy, as I'm perched back on the chair close to the mirror.

She'll try to pull her legs back together but he'll knock them apart again before running his hand over her.

'I don't think you should have taken my panties down,' she'll say in a silly girlish voice.

'Why not? I know you like it when I touch you. You like me touching your pussy like this, don't you?' he'll ask as he gropes between her legs.

'No, I don't,' she'll giggle.

'And what about this?' he'll ask as a finger slips down over her slit.

'I don't like that either,' she'll pout.

'Telling fibs now, are you? I don't like girls who don't tell me the truth. Girls who don't tell the truth deserve to be punished, don't they?'

'Yes,' she'll whisper, fidgeting on his knee.

'If you don't keep still I'll have to tie you up and spank you, you know that, don't you?'

'Yes.'

'Well?'

'I'll keep still,' she'll say.

'Good, now you're showing me you can be a good girl. I won't tie you up this time, but I still have to finish with you.'

Marcus will alternate the spanking, give her one stroke with the ruler, then rub his hand over her arse and give her a sharp slap. Occasionally he'll touch her pussy and I'll watch as she pushes her arse up seductively, obviously wanting more.

*She's such a slut, probably why I love her so much.*

I will want to go in there and give her a spanking myself.

With him holding her like that over his lap, her gorgeous arse beckoning for me to join the party. I'll wait though, not go in, as he doesn't know I'm there and that would spoil our plan.

'Ow,' she'll squeal in pain. 'Stop it. You're hurting. That's too hard.'

'Shut up!' he'll command, hitting her hard on the pussy. 'Quiet, or I'll do it again.'

Rita now stops complaining and starts moaning, making whimpering noises. The smack on her pussy has made her open her legs wider for him. I open mine too, allowing my hand to roam over my pussy noting how wet I am. This is definitely turning me on.

Marcus's hand cups her pussy. She wiggles on his knee, opening her legs wider. I watch as he slips a finger into her hot pussy and then smears her juices over her hole. He opens up her cheeks, teasing her as he probes her hole, just inching in slightly.

*My cheeks clench together as I imagine his finger probing mine.*

'I think you like this, Rita,' Marcus says chuckling. 'Do you think I need to punish you some more?'

'Yes,' she says.

'Come, stand up for me,' he'll say smoothing her skirt over her naked arse. 'That's a good girl. Turn around and face me. That's good. Now take off your skirt.'

Rita has a sly smile on her face as she takes off her skirt. It drops to the floor and she kicks up her other leg, discarding her panties and stands in front of him. Pulling her by the hips he turns her around. He caresses her, lowering his head to kiss her red-hot cheeks. Then he turns her body back around so she is facing him and I note her flushed cheeks. She stares through the glass and smiles, her eyes shining with happiness and excitement.

I've never seen her look so radiant and alive.

'Hmm, very nice,' he'll say, rubbing her stomach, his

38

thumbs pressing into her groin, massaging deep, nearly touching her lips. 'Take off your shirt.'

She undoes each button, teasing him, pouting her lips and looking at him through her dark lashes. Her blouse drops to the floor and she stands there in only a white bra. His hands reach out behind her back, unclasp her bra and discard it on the floor.

Flicking her hair back off her face, she runs her hands over her breasts, down her stomach until she's touching her pussy. She separates the lips and slips her fingers inside. She leans back against the desk, opening her legs.

He kneels down running his tongue over her pussy, giving her a long lick.

'Oh, you're a good girl now, aren't you?' Marcus will say. He'll stand, fondle her breasts and suckle at her nipples. 'You like being a good girl. Don't you?'

She is now only wearing her high-heeled shoes as she wiggles back further on the desk. She lifts a leg and places it over his shoulder. Her heel digging into his back, pulling him in closer.

'Yes,' she'll purr. 'I'm very good when I want to be.'

'Hmm, I know,' he'll say, his fingers seeking out her nipples. 'But there's just one more thing I have to do.'

'What's that?' she'll murmur.

'Lean over the desk'

She doesn't hesitate. She practically pushes him into the glass, turns around and leans into the desk with her arse twitching in the air. Her feet are slightly apart and she lowers herself to lie flat, her breasts squashed against his papers.

Marcus runs his hands over her back, down over her gorgeous plump cheeks, onto her hips which he gives a quick slap, then out of his drawer he'll produce a switch. Gently, he'll begin to whip her, as Rita moans sexily with every lash he administers.

I'll pull my panties to one side, fingering myself on the

armchair; my legs wide open, hanging off the arms. I'll smear my clit with my juices, enjoy my fingers as they roam amongst my folds and then back to my clit where I rub gently, just as I'm doing now.

'That's one hot pussy,' he'll say to Rita as he slips in his finger. 'Oh, yeah, really juicy. You are enjoying it.'

'Oh yeah, baby, I am,' she'll say.

I'll watch as he falls to his knees, lowering his head to lick the welts. He'll run his tongue over them, then her hole, stopping just before he reaches her pussy. She'll rise up on her elbows, pull at her breasts, and tease the nipples to make them erect. She'll push her arse into Marcus's face, lifting it higher, trying to get him to put his tongue inside her.

'That's one hot arse,' he'll laugh as he pinches each cheek. 'Here, stand up.'

He helps her up on the desk. She kneels on it; bends over so her pussy is level with his face. He smacks her thighs with his hand, and as her legs open wider, he smacks her pussy as well. She squeals with delight. He alternates between smacking her and giving her pussy a long lick, from her clit all the way up to her hole. It is driving her wild. She gyrates her pussy into his face, smothering him, encouraging him for more.

It drives me wild too. I can see myself standing and quickly pulling my panties off, re-positioning myself on the chair. I grab at my breast roughly while rubbing my clit. I look sexy, wild and uninhibited as I masturbate madly.

With his free hand he undoes his trousers and they fall to his ankles. He stands there with a massive hard-on. His cock is only inches from me. I can see the knobbly veins in his shaft as the skin stretches tightly over it. I want it, want it in my mouth, in my pussy, my hole. I watch as he covers her pussy with his mouth, nuzzling and sucking while he removes his shirt. Now they are both naked, his arse tight, right in front of me, the cheeks clenching and tightening as he pulls her closer into him.

I'll be rubbing my clit; enjoying a wonderful orgasm as it dribbles out of me, just like I am now. I'll finger myself, focus my attention back on my clit as I rub madly but it won't be enough. I can't get enough. Can't reach the high I want. I need to be fucked and I'll wish that Marcus could be the one to feed my hungry pussy.

He is teasing her with his cock and she's trying desperately to grab it and put it inside her.

'I want your pussy wetter' he'll demand. 'I'll keep spanking you until your juices are dripping on the desk. Do you hear me?'

'Oh, yes, yes,' she'll say eagerly.

He'll slap at her thighs while his cock rubs between her legs. He loves to tease her. Then he'll grab her hips firmly to pull her hard towards him, plunging his cock straight into her pussy; the force of it throws her forward on the desk. He thrust in deeper and harder, causing her to scream and cry out for more. He is holding her tightly, pounding into her ferociously.

'Oh God, yes,' she'll scream. 'Fuck me harder.'

She's holding onto the edges of the desk as he pummels her. Pencils and papers are flying off the desk.

'Quickly,' he'll command. 'Turn around and sit on the desk with your legs open for me.'

She does as he asks. From my position I can see her pussy perfectly. With her legs spread he stands back and pulls at his cock, making it even bigger. She is whimpering, begging for it, her head hanging off the edge of the desk. He thrusts his cock into her open mouth and she gobbles it deep down into her throat, sucking him madly.

'Oh yes, that's great. You're dripping now. I can see your pussy in the mirror. Good girl. I knew you'd be good. Knew you'd do as you're told. Now you'll get your reward,' he'll say, withdrawing from her.

'Oh, yes, Marcus, please. For God's sake, give it to me.'

He pushes his massive cock into her while she screams to be fucked harder. I won't be able to stand it any more and I'll look about the room for something to relieve my frustration. I spy a big, black dildo and reach over to grab it. I hoist up my dress and plunge the black beauty straight into me. Oh, it is heavenly. Over and over I push it in and out. Pulling it out I can see my juices bring it to life, making it seem real.

I'll have my eyes closed on the brink of another orgasm when I hear the creak of a floorboard. He'll be standing next to me, his massive cock only inches from my mouth. I'll grab his shiny, thick, wet shaft and suck his cock deep into my throat. My other hand will still be pumping the dildo in and out and as I gobble his cock. All thoughts about him being Rita's boyfriend will leave me. I will be interested in only one thing and that's getting fucked.

He'll withdraw from me and grab me by the arm, pull me out of the chair. The dildo will fall to the floor. He'll drag me into his bedroom and stand me in front of Rita.

'Lick her pussy,' he'll demand of me.

I'll look slyly towards Rita, knowing that this is what we both want. Like a hungry dog I'll attack her, feed off her juices as Marcus lifts my dress, opens my legs, pulls my hips back and plunges that fucking beautiful cock of his straight up my pussy. I'll grab hold of Rita's hips tightly, licking and sucking as he bucks into me. Delirious with passion I'll come all over his cock as Rita bucks into my mouth, her sweet juices filling me as she too orgasms.

*This fantasy has me masturbating madly as I imagine what else we could do.*

On shaking legs I'll practically fall as Marcus withdraws that wonderful cock from me. He'll strip me out of my dress and underwear and after helping Rita from the desk he'll order me to lie upon it. Apprehensive and nervous about my first caning, I'll lay there panting as they tie my arms and legs to the desk. I'll be hanging over it, my arse and pussy naked, vulnerable, unable to protest even if I want to. But I don't. I want to be spanked, whipped, smacked. I want what Rita had and more.

The first slap will be on my thigh. Then another and another and slowly they'll work their way up to my cheeks where the slaps will become smacks and the stinging pain becomes pleasure. They'll produce a switch and use it over my back, the inside of my torso, my cheeks and thighs. It will be wonderful. It will be absolute and utter pleasure being at the disposal of someone else's hand. I'll love being submissive; to be told what to do and how to do it. I'll love it all.

Then light fingers will run up inside my thighs and caress my back. It will only be a small whip and as Marcus slaps my pussy with it, I'll know that this is something that I'll always want, always want to participate in. The tiny red-hot stings will be like an electrical surge all over my flesh, igniting a fire in me, making me wild with passion.

'Oh, for God's suck, fuck me, please,' I'll beg. 'Fuck me.'

'Do you think you've been punished enough for spying on me?' Marcus will ask.

'Yes,' I'll whimper.

'Do you think you've learn a lesson?' he'll ask.

'Oh, yes,' I'll whisper, barely able to talk.

'Do you think you'd like my cock inside your hot pussy?'

'Oh, fuck, yes. Please fuck me,' I'll beg.

I want him more than anything, but part of me wants them to flip me over. To lash at my breasts, to make my nipples harder, to excite me even more.

'Rita, do you think I should fuck her? Do you think we've shown her how much pleasure you can receive even when you're naughty?'

'I think we've given her enough for her first taste, and knowing Doris, I'm sure she'll be back for more,' Rita will say as she unties my arms, then my legs.

I'll stand on shaking legs, desperate to have Marcus fuck me. He'll lift me in his strong arms and place me in the centre of his bed. Rita will lie beside me, stroking my breasts, lightly touching my arms, while Marcus will stand at the end of the bed watching us.

'Please,' I'll beg, 'I can't stand it any longer. Please fuck me.'

I can hear something pulling at me, digging into my subconscious. I want to continue with this fantasy. I want to imagine Marcus fucking me like the stallion that he is. I want to feel his hard cock deep inside me, I want him pounding in me, fucking me mercilessly, but something is bugging me, stopping me from continuing, my stream of consciousness has been broken.

It's the phone. The fucking phone is ringing. I leave it to ring out but whoever it is rings back. I can't get back into my fantasy. I jump out of bed angrily, rush into the kitchen and snatch the phone off the hook.

'Yes,' I scream into it.

'Julie, is that you?' a voice asks.

'No it's fucking not,' I scream as I slam the receiver back down.

I run to get back to my fantasy, my wild dreams of lust but first I take the receiver off the hook. I don't want any other interruptions.

I jump back into bed. Get into the same position. I close my eyes and conjure up where I'd left off but I can't seem to get it back, can't seem to get the momentum going again. Frustrated and angry I pick up my robe and slink back into my room. I promise myself if Rita brings it up again, I'll be saying yes. This fantasy needs to be fulfilled and the sooner it does the better I'll like it.

# Customer Service
## by Jade Taylor

She couldn't believe Sam's audacity.

She was supposed to be the manager, and fair enough he was the owner of the hotel and she *was* accountable to him, but still.

She wasn't some flunkey low down the chain, she hadn't been the one to fuck up, so why was she the one he sent grovelling?

She'd snapped at Sam, asked if he hadn't somebody who wasn't *quite* as busy, someone who wasn't *quite* so important to send instead.

He'd got irritable then, reminded her that customer service was still part of her job, no matter how high up her position.

It didn't help that Gemma had thought there was something more than a working relationship between them. Twice Sam had asked her out for dinner and they hadn't talked work once, swapping personal details, flirting and getting tipsy instead. Both times she'd been disappointed when the evening ended at her front door, there was no doubt that Sam was a sexy man It was getting way too long since she'd got laid, but she was trying to be understanding, trying to accept that if something happened between them it could make life very complicated.

Well he'd fucked any chance of seeing her naked now. They had enough staff at the hotel specifically employed to deal with customer complaints so that he didn't have to send Gemma with cap in hand. She knew Toshikoe Enterprises was a big corporate client, but so what? Why couldn't they get a letter of apology and a gift basket like every other person did?

Gemma frowned as she took the corner too quickly, her sports car was definitely fast enough to help soothe her temper, but her rage was only going to get worse if she crashed the damn thing.

She had to calm down.

The offices were easy to find, and as Gemma walked in a smart secretary stood immediately to greet her, offering her a drink. Gemma declined, wanting to get this over and done with, and the secretary showed her into the head of Toshikoe Enterprises' office.

The office was large and spacious, with a large dark mahogany desk dominating the room. Gemma had expected some elderly Japanese man, but the man who stood up from behind the desk as she entered definitely wasn't what she was expecting. He was tall and broad shouldered with dark hair and dark eyes, with the haughty arrogance of English aristocracy, and the kind of smile that could be sexy if it wasn't so damn intimidating, so chilling.

He was very sexy.

'Ms Madison, I'm Lord Chatterton, how good of you to come.'

Like she'd had any choice, Gemma thought as she listened to his complaints. They were valid, and as she assured him that they wouldn't happen again, as she offered him discounts and various other incentives to keep his business, she realised that he wasn't actually listening to what she said; he was looking at her legs. They looked good, she knew, in her tight pencil skirt and silk stockings. She'd dressed this morning thinking of Sam, but it looked like it wasn't to be wasted now, as Lord Chatterton blatantly looked her up and down appreciatively.

She caught his gaze, and he licked his lips, smiling.

'Would you like a glass of wine?' he asked, walking over to the drinks cabinet, opening it to display an impressive array of expensive looking bottles. 'Red, I think, a merlot perhaps?'

Red wine made Gemma sleep and slow, but she still nodded; there was something about this man that made it difficult to disagree with him, a presence that commanded compliance.

As he turned away she quickly she undid another two buttons on her blouse, low enough to show a hint of her red bra; if she needed to flirt her way out of this mess it could be an enjoyable way to spend the afternoon.

As he passed her a glass and sat back down Gemma realised that she could see an erection stirring.

Lust flooded through her.

Bad idea, thought Gemma, Sam was mad enough with her already and starting something with a disgruntled customer was hardly going to improve things.

Despite that, as he started flirting with her, talk about the hotel suddenly becoming laden with innuendo, she flirted back, slowly stroking her neck and playing with her hair.

But she could still hardly believe it when he started stroking his hardness through his trousers, his conversation not even faltering.

She was flustered as she drained her drink, trying to summon the courage to say something.

This couldn't be right, could it, even if it were turning her on?

'Lord Chatterton, I don't think this is appropriate,' she told him, but even as she said the words she was watching his cock grow, wondering what it would be like to have him stroke her that way, to feel his thick cock herself.

'I think it's entirely appropriate Ms Madison. Now why don't you make me and your boss a little happier by undoing that blouse a little further.'

She knew she should go, should leave right now, but there was something about him that had her enthralled.

She undid another button.

'Now stand up and bend over my desk,' he commanded, and she blushed immediately.

Protests crowded her mind, she was a thirty-four year old successful woman, a manager of one of the top hotels in the country, he couldn't talk to her like that! There might have been a problem with his booking, but all he was due was an apology, nothing more.

And the look on his face told her exactly what else he was expecting.

She'd never had anybody else look at her like that, so unashamedly lustful, eyes filled with nothing but sex, looking so damn horny.

Despite herself she shivered.

'I said bend over,' he repeated, and this time she did, swallowing the words she'd meant to speak and meekly moving over to his desk.

She bent over.

A moment later he was behind her, caressing her arse through the thin material of her skirt. He moved his hands lower, stroking the back of her thighs, and she heard the catch in his breath as he realised she was wearing stockings and suspenders.

Gemma felt herself flooding with desire, and moved her legs wider apart.

She felt him tug at her skirt, and without saying a word she moved his hips so that he could pull it up more easily. The silence only made the sensations more erotic, as if speaking too were forbidden.

The whole thing felt so deliciously forbidden.

Beneath her skirt she was wearing flimsy French knickers and suspenders, and as he saw them she felt him move closer to her, felt his cock twitch as it grew harder yet.

He had her so confused she didn't know whether she felt more scared or more turned on, but the ache between her legs was so strong she knew she couldn't walk away, so strong that she knew she'd do whatever he demanded.

Then he spanked her.

It was only once, not hard but enough to make her bum tingle, to make her wriggle away slightly. She stopped as he placed his hand on the back of her neck to hold her down; it wasn't hard enough to stop her moving away but still she complied with his unspoken demand.

I should say something, Gemma thought, there could be anyone outside his office, anyone could walk in on us like this, I'm letting this man I don't even know *spank* me.

He waited for her to say something, for her to burst into outraged tears or worse, outraged swearing, for some complaint, but she said nothing. Her passivity was as much of a turn on as the situation, and he felt his cock pulsing with heat.

He spanked her again, his cock feeling twice the size of normal, hard and heavy.

Gemma said nothing, her panties getting damper, her cunt getting slick and swollen as if ready already to accommodate him, ready for him to easily slide inside her.

She wondered if he would fuck her.

'Take off your panties,' he told her, releasing her. She should say no she thought, should tell him about the two hundred member of staff working beneath her, about the important decisions she made daily, about how she was in control of her life and wouldn't relinquish her power so easily to him.

But submission was suddenly so much more appealing, so much sexier.

Instead she stood upright to shimmy out of her panties, pulling her skirt down to cover her modesty even as she stepped out of the material gathered around her ankles to resume her position meekly at his desk.

He could smell her arousal now, the scent of her sexuality, and knew that this was turning her on as much as it was him. He licked his lips, wishing he could taste her musky scent, but enjoying himself too much to stop what he was doing.

Maybe some other time.

He slapped her arse again, thinking of her the bare skin beneath, of her wetness, of the slick scent of her.

He couldn't stop himself now, pulling up her skirt even as she murmured her protests but didn't actually try to stop him, wanting to see her bare arse, so deliciously presented in the frame of stockings and suspenders. Such an old fashioned touch, but so utterly exciting.

He stroked her arse softly, taking in the redness, the way she wriggled beneath his touch, watching as her legs instinctively moved apart so her heady perfume filled the air once more.

The chill air meeting her arse only served to make it feel more sensitive, and as he began stroking her Gemma felt the flaming sensation on her arse spread further around her cunt, making her wish he would stroke her clit.

Instead he slapped her hard, and she cried out with a mixture of shock and desire.

He'd left a handprint this time, and he traced the outline of it with his finger, stroking her sensitive skin, before letting his fingers slide further down.

Again he spanked her, feeling the heat rising from her arse now as he caressed it, then slid a finger lower down into her wetness, hearing her breathing quicken as he stroked her clit.

Now Gemma sighed, she felt like her arse was on fire as well as her cunt, the ache of the slaps mingling with the ache of desire, each intensifying the other. She knew this wasn't right, to be lying like this with her bare arse up in the air in his office where anybody could be outside as she let him spank her, but she couldn't stop him now; not because of Sam telling her to fix the problem but because she knew that this ache in her must be satisfied.

She couldn't believe how wet she felt, that her breasts felt so sensitive, her nipples so hard, her whole body tingling.

He slapped her again, feeling like his cock would burst if it wasn't released soon, thinking of how he would love to slide it in her as his fingers slid inside her, as he rubbed her clit so that she gasped and writhed against him, so close to release.

He moved slightly, reaching in his drawer for his hand cream. Slowly he squirted it across her reddened cheeks, and then rubbed it into her sensitive arse, alternating the soothing touch with a slap and then a stroke of her clit.

He wanted her so badly.

As Gemma writhed against his touch she felt that she would let him do anything to her now that he wanted, she was so horny her juices were dribbling down her thighs, she wanted to come so much. If he asked to fuck her up the arse now she knew she'd have no choice to say yes, she was completely under his control. Instead he continued to tease, to stroke, to soothe, to spank.

Gemma could feel her orgasm approaching, and though she was almost ashamed of the way she'd reached it, of having subjugated herself to this stranger in his office, of having him slap her arse before touching her so intimately, she knew she couldn't stop it. The feeling was too intense and she couldn't stop it as desire shook her body, waves of heat throbbing inside her until she had to bite her lip to stop herself crying out madly.

He smiled as she came, glad she'd been satisfied. He moved away as at last he undid his trousers to release his swollen cock, the muskiness of his scent filling the room. It was already wet around the tip and he used the wetness to lubricate his cock, grabbing it hard as he stroked up and down, reaching for a condom and fumbling as he put it on, so desperate to be inside her at last.

Quickly he plunged inside her, her wetness meaning he slid inside easily, smiling as she started touching herself, as her breathing started getting as quick as his was, as he felt her muscles clenching hard around his cock as she came once more, seeming to milk him as he moaned loudly, his orgasm consuming him in heat.

For a moment neither said anything, then he moved away to dispose of the condom, to allow her to pull back on her panties, to straighten her clothes.

Still breathless and flushed she asked, 'I assume that concludes our business Lord Chatterton?'

He laughed, a deep boom of a laugh that surely would have people outside wondering what was happening inside, if they weren't already.

'I'd say that business had been concluded most satisfactorily. And maybe you would call me Edward?'

He held out his hand.

'Gemma,' she replied, shaking his hand.

Sam phoned her as she was soaking in the bath, her skin still sensitive and her arse still sore.

'I wondered if you'd like to go out later? The client was very pleased with you.'

So he fucking should be, Gemma thought, but she'd known that by the flowers that had just arrived, by the invite out to dinner.

By the invite to explore her darker side further.

'I have plans,' she told him; now she'd been with Edward she knew Sam would prove too boring.

'Okay, well, well done,' Sam told her, obviously miffed.

'All part of the service,' she told him, sinking back into the bath and her fantasies of what might happen next.

# Grip
## by Sommer Marsden

'Jesus, Annalee, what have you done?'

Jacob stared at my hair and I tried not to shift. It was my hair. I could cut it any way I wanted. I would not feel bad. The only reason he was pissed was a small reason. Ninety-five percent of the time he didn't give a shit about my hair. Not the colour, not the style, not any of it. It was that five percent of the time that my hair was cherished.

'I like it,' I sighed. 'Look, don't get pissy. I needed something new and I went ahead and did it. You'll get used to it.' I set about making dinner, intent on ending the turmoil right then and there.

'But you know how much I love your hair. Loved,' he corrected himself. There was venom in both the statement and the tone.

'You love it when you fuck me,' I sniped. 'More specifically, you love it when you fuck me from behind. You like to twist it up around your fist and yank me back with it. Yes, Jacob, I love that, too. However,' I banged the stock pot down and cringed at the loud noise, 'during the times when you are not playing caveman and using my hair as a reign, it's a pain in the ass!'

We stood there, eyeing each other in the kitchen, both of us angry, both of us thinking we were right. He could think he was right. That was fine. But it was my damn hair and I

53

was sick of the work and the struggle of keeping a waist length mane clean, detangled and neat. I liked the new hair; just below chin level, layered to be shaggy but not messy. I threw my shoulders back. No guilt.

'I'm sorry if you don't like it but you'd better adjust. I am not growing it back out and I will not apologise for doing it.' Then I turned my back on him and started the water to boil.

Jacob barely spoke to me for three days. Every time I said or did the slightest thing he didn't approve of he would pause for several beats and stare at my hair. As if to say; look what you have done.

While he was busy frowning upon my new 'do, I was falling more and more in love with it. No more long mornings steaming myself in front of the mirror with a blazing hot hair dryer. No more combing out knots so big and stubborn I ended up in tears holding a fist full of my own hair. No more torture, muss, fuss and annoyance. It was freedom, this wonderful short flirty hair. I loved it enough for both of us.

Needless to say, it was a while before I got laid. Without my crowning glory of long chocolate coloured hair, I seemed to have lost my appeal. Or so it seemed.

The first time Jacob stooped to touching my new hair was the night of his boss's dinner party. Stewart J. Beckett was a prick and a blow hard and he loved my husband. We were expected to attend dinner. We were expected to be amusing and classy. We were expected to dress the part.

I straightened my taupe and black wrap dress. I fidgeted with the black satin collar for the millionth time. I flipped the cuffs up to show the black satin. I flipped them down to create bell sleeves. Designers who make dresses that can be worn several different ways should be shot. Do they not realise that the woman wearing their dress will most likely be a nervous wreck, which will result in her having absolutely no decision making skills? Black cuffs, bell sleeves, black cuffs…

Jacob took pity on me. 'Leave them flipped up. Let the cuffs match the collar.' Then he put his arms around my waist, temporarily it seemed forgetting my traitorous behaviour. 'You look stunning, by the way. It'll be fine. We'll eat, we'll be fake, we'll leave. Plead a headache the moment dessert arrives,' he chuckled, then kissed my ear.

He did not smooth his hands over the length of my hair as he normally did when we were about to go out. Of course, the length itself was gone.

'Time to go,' he sighed and pulled my hand. 'We'll make it as quick as possible.'

'My necklace!' I raced back in and grabbed the antique necklace he had given me for Christmas. It complimented the vintage nature of the dress. My hands were shaking just thinking about Miriam Beckett. Such a prude, such a bitch. I felt sick.

'Let me.' He draped the necklace at the hollow of my throat and clasped it. Then he kissed the nape of my neck. That spot. It gets me every time. I froze and let the pleasant tickle and tingle run down my spine.

Then his hands were in my hair. Shoving up under the chunky layers along my neck. His fingers slid up to rest below my ears, which made me shiver. He sifted my newly shorn hair through his big fingers and I heard him make a low sound. A pleased sound? I wasn't sure. Then he gripped a fistful of my hair at the base of my head and tugged ever so slightly. I gasped and felt my nipples bead against my silk bra.

'Time to go,' he said again but this time his voice was a little thicker. A little slower.

We went.

Somehow, all through dinner, all I could think about was how it felt when Jacob gripped my hair and pulled. How it was pleasingly painful. When I closed my eyes I could feel

55

it; a phantom sensation of him yanking me by my short stylish hair. By dessert, I couldn't stop shifting in my seat. My panties were damp, I was bored beyond belief and all I wanted was to get home so I could find out what it felt like when he pulled my hair like that with his cock buried deep inside me.

'I have a migraine!' I blurted with only two spoonfuls of sorbet under my belt. What I really had was a soaking wet cunt and an overwhelming urge to run screaming from the boredom.

'I'd better get you home then,' Jacob said gallantly and mumbled his thanks and goodbyes.

I was the only one who noticed his subtle smile. Or the way his eyes flashed with a hunger that had nothing to do with dessert.

We didn't speak on the drive home. Jacob piloted the car with one hand. The other was perpetually in my hair. Twirling, yanking, sifting. The only sound I made resembled the purr of a content feline.

In the house, he was deliberate. He hung up our coats, checked the door, fiddled with the thermostat. I waited. It was all I could do to keep from hiking up my dress and demanding his services right then and there. I knew better. The waiting made the event more exciting. The waiting was the foreplay.

Without a word, he took my hand and firmly led me up the steps. He bent, removed my shoes and put them neatly to the side. Standing together. The heels aligned as perfectly as if on display in a shop window.

Then the stockings. Then the tie of the dress. When he pulled the second tie, he finally spoke, 'I love taking you out of one of these things. It's like unwrapping a present.'

I didn't say anything. I swallowed and my throat clicked. My heart hurt it was beating so hard. My eyelids shut and I hummed aloud as he dragged his warm hands over the flat of my belly and then hooked my panties with his thumbs

56

and pushed them down. His mouth gave my pussy just enough attention to leave it wanting. Just a few delicate tastes of my sensitive flesh. A few flicks to my swollen clit. Then he continued his trail upward as I shivered and shook and fought the urge to beg. He bit my nipples through the lace cups of my bra as he unhooked it, then, lowering it with dramatic care, he hung it on the knob of my bedside table drawer. Each breast received its reward. Each nipple tortured into perfect tautness. And when I was shifting and breathing in little fits and gasps, he spun me and pushed me to the bed.

'How wet are you now, Annalee? I bet you're gushing. I bet I could stick all of my fingers into that perfect pink cunt. Should I try or do you want something else from me?'

I whimpered.

He pushed me so my upper body was bowed against the mattress, my ass in the air. I sighed, this was how I liked to be. Held down by him. Taken. Overpowered. He slid his hand along my neck as the other was busy with my cunt, my clit. He shoved his hand into my hair and gripped a nice fistful tugging to the precise level of pain I like and slid a thick finger into my ass. I bucked under him, fire spreading from my hair to my ass, flowing like quicksilver into my soaking sex. I wanted to plead with him but I knew better.

'You want something else. I know you do. If I stare at your pussy, I can see it moving. Greedy, greedy girl. It contracts and expands like it's dancing.' Jacob laughed and I heard the smacks echo through the room before I felt them. Then the fire set in. The burn of sharp cracks of open palm to the soft flesh of my bottom. He yanked my hair and with the combined pain I felt a warm slow trickle slide down my inner thighs.

His finger wiped some up. I heard him lick his finger and laugh. With a final tug to the tender roots of my hair he shoved into me. His hips banging me mercilessly, driving me into the mattress as he gripped me with the most fragile part of my body. My scalp sang with pain even as my cunt tightened around him. The agony in my scalp making the pleasure that flowed nearly to my womb that much more sweet.

More smacks and I bowed under him as much as physically possible, my body demanding release even as my soul relished the torture.

'I say three,' Jacob ground out the words. His voice was heavy and thick. His hips moving faster. He was going to come.

I would go with him.

'One!' he shouted out and I could tell he was fighting for control. My body jerked and my cunt grew tighter. 'Two!' The sensation of tension. The heavy feeling of almost release. 'Three!' he bellowed with the final blow and a perfect painful yank to my scalp.

I came. A great spiralling orgasm that had me sobbing under his bucking body. Fire and light and pain and pleasure became one as I let go and fell into it. No body, no time. Nothing. A single nerve ending singing with unbearable pleasure. That was all I was for that moment in time.

Jacob fell against me, helping me to lower myself flat on my stomach. He laid on me, crushing the breath from my lungs but I liked it. The fingers that had just yanked and tortured, smoothed along my scalp in soothing circles. I felt the mattress wet beneath my face. I was crying. I usually did.

Jacob kissed the nape of my neck. Bare, naked, and on display for him at all hours now that my curtain of hair was gone. His cock had gone soft inside of me but we stayed that way. Connected.

'I owe you an apology, Annalee,' he laughed in my ear. His hand found my breast and gave a possessive squeeze.

'Oh yeah?'

'I love your new hair,' he chuckled again and then gave my nipple a twist.

I gasped and squirmed under him and then I was laughing. 'Thank you. I knew you'd come around.'

# My Lord's Rump
## by Chloe Devlin

'C'mon, babe. Please.'

Angie rolled away from George, slipping out from under his caressing fingers. 'I don't think so,' she replied. 'You know I'm not into that sort of thing.'

'It's not like I'm going to stick my prick up your ass,' he protested. 'Just my finger. Just to play with your asshole a little bit. It'll feel great.'

'Yeah, and before I know it, I'll have your dick buried in my rump. No, thanks.' She dragged the covers up to her chest, reaching down to the foot of the bed where they'd flung them.

George stood, pointing an imperious finger. He'd abruptly switched into one of the role-playing games they occasionally used. 'I am your liege and you shall obey me.'

For a split second, she thought about using their 'out' word. But in two years of their games, she'd never had to use it. And she wouldn't use it now. She knew George wouldn't hurt her.

Falling in line with his fantasies, she rolled over and crouched on all fours, looking over her shoulder at her naked lover standing beside the bed, his aroused cock jutting forward. 'My lord, I am yours to command,' she said, tentatively. 'But I beg you to remember that I am still a virgin back there and very tight. I fear that even your finger will be too large for me.'

'Never fear, dear maiden. Your pleasure is my only wish,' he vowed before going into the bathroom. While he was gone, Angie grabbed a few pillows, using them to prop her abdomen up. Might as well get comfortable, she thought.

When he returned, he set the tube of KY on the nightstand, before reaching into the bedside drawer for a set of leather cuffs.

'Dear maiden,' he said. 'Knowing your... er... maidenly fears, I believe you should wear these cuffs so that you won't be tempted to stop your liege's pleasure.'

Angie didn't even hesitate this time. If she was honest with herself, the thought of George's finger sliding up her rump was starting to get her excited.

She stretched out her arms in front of her, allowing him to buckle the cuffs around her wrists, then fasten them together to the headboard.

'One more thing,' he said, then clipped the ankle cuffs on her, fastening the metal buckles together. 'Now you're ready for me.'

Angie felt compelled to issue one more reminder. 'My lord,' she began, then shifted her weight as George guided her hips to where he wanted them. She felt something cool being rubbed around her anus.

'That's it, dear maiden,' George said. 'That's the perfect position for me to play. Let me rub the outside for a little bit. I like the way your asshole crinkles around the edges.'

As he touched her pucker, she clenched her muscles then relaxed them. It was kind of strange to hear George describing what she was feeling – somehow surprising. She was surprising herself, it seemed.

As he explored, he kept up a running commentary. 'Tight skin. Smooth, but it blends nicely with the folds here. And look. Your cheeks are rounded like a pear.' He massaged the two globes with his other hand, kneading the flesh. 'They fall apart when you crouch like that. Nice. I can concentrate on your pretty little asshole.'

Angie buried her head in her pillow, closing her eyes. The fresh scent of clean sheets filled her nostrils, making her glad she'd changed the bed linen earlier that day. Images of what George was doing flashed behind her eyelids, adding to the wash of sensations in her butt. Using just the tip of his blunt forefinger, he penetrated her asshole slightly, wiggling inside. She felt the movement on all sides of her rectum, a nice rubbing that was getting her excited.

'Oh, dear maiden,' he crooned. 'You're so tight. So virginal. You're squeezing the cream on my finger out around my whole hand. But you're still hot and wet inside.'

As he went further, she clenched her muscles around the invader. She could feel the base of his hand resting against the damp lips of her pussy. She tightened several times, liking the strange fullness as he inserted more of his finger inside.

'That's right, babe. Squeeze me tight.' George lost his role and his voice grew hoarse. 'Grab my finger. If you'd let me stick my prick up your butt, you'd be nice and tight.'

She flinched, but he continued soothing her as he gently pumped his finger in and out of her butt. 'I know. I know. Don't worry. I won't go back on my word. I won't stick my cock in your ass. Well, not unless you beg me.'

He slid his other hand off her butt cheek and ran a finger through her wet pussy lips, spreading them apart, then tickling the sensitive flesh as she gushed with juices. 'I would know how it feels,' he said. 'Tell me, fair maid, what my finger in your ass feels like.'

Speak? When she could hardly catch her breath? A moan escaped her when his fingertip pressed against her clit.

'Ah, I know you like that, fair maiden. You have one of the most sensitive clits I've ever seen.'

Shivers of excitement darted throughout her body. 'Seen many?' she whispered. 'Clits, I mean?'

He didn't bother to answer her question. 'Yours is the best. Just like your ass.'

'Glad you like it.' Her words ended on a moan as he resumed gently pumping her asshole. He was kind of doing the rub-your-head, pat-your-tummy thing with his two fingers. One was sliding in and out of her butt while the other gently circled her tingling clit.

When she moaned again, he ordered, 'Now tell me. I command you. What does it feel like?'

'Full.' She sighed. 'God, it makes me want to push out. Then tighten up and pull you in.'

She wiggled her butt, trying to get more of his probing finger inside. 'Oh, God. That's it,' she yelped. 'Right there.'

He moved his finger in and out faster. 'Do you want more? Maybe another finger?'

She hadn't expected to get this hot with his finger in her butt, but she wasn't just damp between her legs, she was drenched with her excitement.

She grabbed the headboard tightly and rocked back against his hand. 'Yessss…' The word was torn from her as she gasped for breath. 'Another finger. In each hole. No, two more!'

He complied, simultaneously pumping both hands in and out, stretching her wide open. 'Oh, my lord,' she groaned, feeling her lust rising. 'You're gonna make me come. I can't believe it.'

He bent down and nipped at her ass cheek as he continued his two-handed finger-fucking. 'Believe it, baby. I knew you'd like getting fucked in the ass. You're so anal-sensitive.'

The playful bite pushed her over the edge. She started to spasm as her orgasm rolled over her. 'Oh God! That's it. Don't stop! Make me come!'

George continued to shove his fingers in and out, switching to an alternating rhythm. She felt the fire race through her body as she arched her back, trying to get as much of his hand into her ass as she could. She shuddered all over as she continued to come from the dual stimulation, her mouth open as she stiffened and strained against the intense pleasure.

Finally, his fingers slowed their movement until he was rubbing her asshole with one fingertip and her clit with another. She panted, nearly hyperventilating, as she collapsed onto her stomach.

George withdrew his fingers and bent over her, licking lazy designs on her butt cheeks. 'Like that, baby?'

She sighed, still gulping for air, her heart still pounding. 'It was fantastic, George. I never dreamed... If you promise not to say 'I told you so', I just might ask you to butt-fuck me.'

'My lips are sealed.'

Realising they'd fallen out of their role-playing, she twisted to the side so she could see his face over her shoulder. 'My lord, the experience was everything you claimed it would be. It has aroused such a passion in me that I beg of you to fuck my ass.'

He managed to remain calm and in character, gently stroking her sweaty body. 'I believe such an event can be arranged, dear maiden.'

'Thank you, my lord.' She rested her cheek against the pillow, the cotton soft against her hot skin. 'I feel shame that I ever doubted you. If there is anything I could do to make it up to you...' She let her voice trail off suggestively.

A broad palm abruptly came down on one ass cheek, the smack tingling her flesh. 'Anything?' George murmured, his hand upraised again.

She glanced over to his unbending erection, a drop of pre-cum pearling at the tip. Her mouth watered and arousal flowed through her body, giving her courage. 'Anything you wish, my lord.'

As he regally nodded, then broke character and gave a whoop, she allowed him to pull her back onto all fours.

'What a lucky lord you are to have such an adventurous maiden.'

# My Therapist In Action
## by Eva Hore

I'd forgotten the shopping that I'd left by my seat after my session with my new therapist. I've been suffering from depression, he was suggested to me by my friend Mary, who had been seeing him regularly for the last six months.

It was late, after seven, but I knew the code to the door and didn't think he'd mind me waiting in the reception area if he was with a patient.

The guy was gorgeous. No wonder Mary couldn't wait for her Friday sessions. Anyway, I was walking past his office window when I heard his voice and Mary's. Being nosy by nature, I hung back, wanting to hear if he said the same sort of things to her that he did to me.

He was very big on role-playing to build up your confidence.

'Hi, Mary,' Michael was saying. 'Good to see you. Just take a seat; I'll only be a minute.'

'Thanks, you're looking well,' she purred.

After a few moments of silence his voice was firm and controlled.

'Right. Today we'll do-role play with you as an employee and I'll be your boss, OK?' Michael said.

I noticed an old milk crate resting beside the back door and pulled it over so I could stand on it and see into his office.

'If that's what you think we should do,' she said, quietly.

I had the perfect view. I was able to look down on them. Perfect for spying.

'Your boss, Marcus McManus, is the company director, OK?'

'Okay,' she said.

'You've been unfair to some staff members and he's called you into the office. OK, you ready to begin?'

'Sure.'

'I hear you've been bullying some of our employees,' he said in a firm voice.

'I wouldn't say that,' she said defensively.

'Mary, the idea of this treatment is to put you in a vulnerable position,' Michael was saying patiently. 'This is to give you an idea of the fear people feel when they're subjected to an over-zealous boss who loves power. For this to work I need you to feel submissive. In order for that to come about, you have to do everything I say without question and participate as though it really is you being threatened. Understand?'

'I think so,' she said.

'You don't mind if I have the tape going do you? I always think it's good to look back on. See how you react to certain situations.'

'No, that's fine,' she said, re-crossing her long legs.

'Remember what we spoke about in our last session. It's important for you to try to imagine yourself as just an employee while we play out your therapy.'

'Okay,' she nodded respectfully.

'I heard you've been disobedient, Mary.'

'I... I don't know what to say, Doctor.'

'Mary, I'm not the doctor now. We're role-playing. You're only to address me as sir. Speak as though you're just one of the employees. Let's begin again. Your supervisor told me you've been giving him cheek, and he sent you in for me to deal with.'

68

'Well, he's always picking on me. I can't do anything right, by him.'

'That's good, keep it up.'

'He's had it in for me since I started,' she said, smiling slyly at him.

'Come here so I can punish you. Come close and bend over my knee.'

'No, sir. Please, I promise to try harder.'

She stayed in the chair.

'Do you like being called into my office?'

'No, sir, I don't.'

'Then why haven't you come over here like I asked?'

'Sorry, sir,' she went over and stood in front of him with her hands folded.

'You've been rude and I have to punish you. Bend over my knee.'

Giggling, she bent over his knee. He pulled up her skirt and started to spank her on the bum. When she didn't respond he spanked her harder.

'Oww,' she cried.

'That's what happens when you don't do as you're told,' Michael said.

'Sir, you're hurting me,' she whined. 'Please stop. I promise I'll behave.'

Michael kept on hitting her, slapping his hand backwards and forwards, ignoring her pleas.

'That's hurting,' she said loudly, looking over at the camera.

'It's supposed to hurt, Mary. You've been disobedient, and all disobedient employees need to be punished,' Michael said, lifting her skirt higher and pulling her panties down, exposing red cheeks.

I gasped. I couldn't believe what I was watching.

He rubbed his hands over her bum, caressing it with circular motions. Then he ran his finger down the crack, over her hole, up and down. Kneading her cheeks, he

69

opened them and inspected her, before sliding his finger further towards her pussy.

She moved her hands, trying to cover her bum. He smacked her hands away. She squirmed trying to get up, but he held her down.

'You're hurting me!'

'You shouldn't have put your hands there. You know the rules. Now I'll have to spank you with the ruler.'

What? What on earth was he doing?

'I get what you mean, doctor. I think I've had enough,' she said, turning her head to speak to him.

'I'm your boss, not a doctor. The second rule is no talking. Now I'm going to have to spank you harder.'

I could see her bum getting even redder as he hit her with a ruler. He expertly slipped her panties down to her ankles, sliding them off one leg and left them dangling on the other. With his free hand he pushed her legs apart, giving himself a nice view of her pussy.

'Sir, please don't,' she pleaded, trying to pull her legs back together.

'I said no talking, Mary. You like being bad, don't you?' he said, forcing her legs back open.

'No, I don't, sir. I don't think you should have taken my panties down. I'll tell Mrs McManus,' she said in a pathetic voice.

'Rule number three, Mary. What happens in this room stays in this room. I only want to help you. I want you to learn respect. You don't want to get the sack do you?'

'No, sir, I don't.'

Michael alternated the spanking, giving her one stroke with the ruler, then rubbing his hand over her bum to give her a sharp slap. Occasionally, he'd touch her pussy. I noticed she didn't seem to mind, even pushing her bum up seductively, as though encouraging him.

How dare he! Using his position as a therapist to get his rocks off. And Mary! How could she believe this was therapy? She was as bad as he was.

'Ow,' she squealed in pain. 'Stop it. My bum's going numb. You're hitting too hard.'

'Shut up!' he commanded, hitting her hard on the pussy. 'Shut up or I'll do it again.'

Mary stopped complaining and started moaning, making whimpering noises. Now she actually seemed to be enjoying it. The smack on her pussy made her open her legs wider for him.

'I think you like this, Mary,' Michael said chuckling. 'Do you think I need to punish you some more?'

'Yes, sir,' she said.

'Come on; stand up for me,' he said, smoothing her skirt over her naked bum. 'That's a good girl. Turn around and take off your skirt.'

Mary had a sly smile on her face and took off her skirt without hesitation. She kicked up the other leg, discarding her panties and stood there in front of him. He turned her around slowly rubbing his hands over her.

When she was facing him again he caressed her stomach, travelling slowly downwards until he touched her pubic hair.

'You've got lovely red hair there, haven't you? Oh, and a little further down there's some more on your pussy lips. Hmm, it's a nice pussy isn't it? Come and let me see the rest of you,' he said, moving his hands under her blouse.

She undid each button, teasing him as she went, pouting her lips and looking up at him through her lashes. Her blouse dropped to the floor and she stood there in only a white bra.

I couldn't believe my eyes. I looked about; making sure no one was watching me.

Now Michael ran his fingers over the lace on the bra and forced her breasts up so they hung out over the top.

'Such lovely breasts,' he said, fondling them and giving the nipples a quick suck.

Fuck, I was getting horny just watching. I wondered if he'd ever do this to me.

Giggling she ran her hands down her stomach, touching her pussy, separating the lips and slipping her fingers inside. She leaned back against the desk, opening her legs further making sure her pussy was more visible for his eyes.

He knelt down to run his tongue over her pussy, giving her a long lick.

My pussy throbbed as I imagined him doing that to me.

'Good girl,' Michael said, standing again, tweaking her nipples. 'You like being a good girl. Don't you?' he said un-clipping her bra and letting it fall to the floor with the rest of her clothes. All she was wearing now were her high-heeled shoes.

'Yes, sir,' she said.

'Lean over the desk so I can punish you some more.'

She didn't hesitate. Totally nude she leaned on the desk with her bum twitching in the air, her feet slightly apart. She shook her hair seductively and looked long and hard into the camera.

Michael stood and got a switch out of his drawer. It looked like it was made of bamboo. Gently he began to whip her.

'Oh, sir, don't,' she said, looking at him with her tongue running along her top lip.

She didn't sound too convincing to me.

Smirking, Michael spread her legs wider so he could see her pussy and started whipping a bit harder. She must have gotten a shock that he hit her so hard because she put her hands behind, to protect herself again.

'Didn't I tell you not to do that?'

'I'm, sorry, sir but you're really hurting me.'

'It's supposed to hurt, but I think you like it. You like me punishing you, don't you?'

'No, I don't,' she said.

'Yes, you do. I can see your pussy and it's getting wet,' he said rubbing his hand over it. 'Hmm, yes it is. You are enjoying this Mary.'

'No, sir, I'm not. Honestly.'

'Well that's not what your pussy's telling me. Look, it's getting really juicy now,' he said slipping in his finger. 'Oh, yeah, really juicy. You are enjoying it.'

'I'm not,' she said, even though she was holding his hand there.

Her bum was moving towards his crotch as he withdrew his fingers, smearing her juices over the crack of her bum. She moaned, lifting it even higher towards him.

I pressed my thighs together but that only made my pussy pulsate more. I was torn between wanting to leave, to go home and masturbate, and staying and continuing to watch, to see just how far they'd go.

I watched as Michael fell to his knees, lowering his head to lick at the welts. He ran his tongue over them, then her hole, stopping just before her pussy.

She was up on her elbows now, pulling at her breasts, grabbing at the nipples, probably to make them erect as she pushed her bum into Michael's face, lifting it higher, trying to get his tongue inside her.

Suddenly he stood and looked down at her. I thought it might have been over.

'That's one hot bum,' he said laughing, pinching each cheek.

I watched him rub at his crotch before helping her up, getting her up on the desk. She knelt and bent over so her pussy was level with his face.

Michael began to smack her thighs with his hand, and as her legs were now wide open he smacked her pussy as well. She squealed with delight. He alternated between smacking her and giving her pussy a long lick, from her clit all the way up to her hole. It was driving her wild. She was gyrating her pussy into his face, encouraging him for more.

I slipped my hand between my legs, rubbing through the fabric of my skirt and panties. With his free hand he undid his trousers and they fell to his ankles. He stood there looking ridiculous with his cock hanging out. He covered her pussy with his mouth nuzzling and sucking. With his other hand he removed his shirt. Now they were both naked.

I was shocked at my reaction to this sort of humiliation but couldn't tear myself away.

Michael had his face smothered in her and she was bent over moaning and grabbing her breasts. Her head flung upwards, her breathing coming in gasps.

Grabbing her hips he pulled her back over the edge of the desk and pushed her roughly, face down, onto it. Papers and pencils flew onto the floor.

He held her firmly in this position, his cock resting between her cheeks. He began smacking her thighs again and I could see how red her bum was. It looked like he'd broken the skin but she seemed oblivious to it. She was really getting off on this.

'Spread your legs and do what I tell you,' he said.

'Oh, yes, sir. Anything. I'll do anything you say. I'll be a good girl, I promise,' Mary said, her passion obvious from her voice.

He parted her cheeks, rubbing his cock over her hole and pussy. He was wetting his cock, teasing her pussy by just putting it in a fraction and then pulling back.

'Fuck me, sir. Oh please, fuck me now,' she begged.

He continued to tease her with his cock while she desperately tried to grab at it and put it inside her.

'I want your pussy wetter, do you hear me?' he demanded.

'Yes, sir, yes,' she squealed, thrashing her head from side to side.

74

He stood back and started hitting her cheeks harder. She cried out for him to stop but this only seemed to excite him further.

She turned her face and looked at him over her shoulder. I could see tears flowing freely but still she continued to push her bum up to greet each new smack.

He grabbed her pussy hard, 'Oh, yeah, Mary. You are so wet.' He was pulling at her pubic hair and sticking his fingers inside, 'Hmm, you like me punishing you don't you?'

'Yes, sir, yes,' she said in between sobs.

He grabbed her hips firmly, pulling her hard towards him, plunging his cock straight into her pussy, the force of it throwing her forward on the desk. He thrust in deeper and harder, making her scream and cry out for more. He was holding her hips, pounding into her ferociously.

'Quickly,' he commanded, 'turn around and sit on the desk with your legs open wide.'

She did as she was told and I knew why he'd asked her. From this angle the camera would be focused right on her pussy. I wondered how many other times he'd done this to her, or other patients. If he'd ever try and do it to me.

With her legs spread wide he stood back and pulled at his cock, making it even bigger. She was whimpering, begging for it. He stood beside her, roughly pushing and prodding her pussy, telling her it wasn't wet enough. She bucked her hips up wildly, throwing her legs further apart so that they were hanging off the side of the desk, begging him for more.

I could feel myself getting more and more excited too. I moved my hand down inside my panties and felt my pussy. It was wet. Really wet. I slipped a finger in, then another as I tried to balance on the crate to locate my clit. It was already hard. I rubbed it quickly enjoying the sensation.

I wiggled out of my panties, dropping them onto the ground. I watched, fascinated now with what was going on, even giving my own pussy a smack to see what it felt like. It began to swell as blood rushed around and I slipped my fingers inside, noticing that I too was definitely wetter.

'Good girl,' he said. 'Now open your mouth. Wider,' he commanded, as he pushed his cock in.

This threw her into a frenzy. She squirmed and bucked on that desk as he rammed his fingers inside her, finger fucking her while she sucked his cock, loudly slurping and choking on it as he pushed himself further into her mouth.

I rubbed my clit harder, getting hotter and hotter. I finger fucked myself, reaching a high I hadn't felt for a long time, as I watched them, pretending they were putting on a show just for me.

It seemed to go on forever before he turned her around, slamming her face down on the desk again; grabbing both legs to pull them wide apart and ramming his cock into her hole. She went wild, pulling him into her, matching his thrusts as he plunged into her over and over.

I frantically rubbed myself, my fingers massaging my clit, bringing me to a powerful orgasm as I watched him yank her backwards, grabbing at her breasts roughly, pinching her nipples so hard she actually yelled out for him to stop. There was no way he'd be stopping, even I knew that. I touched my own breasts, fondling them, teasing the nipples until they too were erect.

Finally, he pulled his cock out of her and sprayed his come over her face and breasts. She loved it. I watched her smear it into her mouth, licking and sucking it off her fingers.

He moved away from her, quickly dressing, while she lay there, battered and bruised, legs still wide open.

'Here,' he said, handing her her crumpled clothes. 'Get dressed. The session's over.'

'What…'

She looked a little bit shocked at his attitude, and with her legs visibly shaking, she got off the desk and slowly began to put her clothes back on.

My legs were shaking too as this brought me back to reality. I quickly jumped off the crate and retrieved my panties, pulling them on over my saturated pussy. I couldn't believe what I'd just done. Masturbated in the dark like this and out in the open. Scrambling over the crate, I hurried into the waiting room, trying hard to stop my racing heart.

'Mary, please,' he said. I could hear him through the door as I sat primly in the waiting room. 'I only did this for you to show you how it feels to be submissive to someone in authority. Do you think it helped?'

'What…' she mumbled. 'I thought that maybe…' she left the rest unsaid.

'You thought what? I told you before this session began that I was doing this purely to help you in order that you achieve a perspective of how it feels when you're vulnerable to another person. I'm sure we've succeeded in that, don't you agree? If not come back and see me in a month and we'll discuss it again.'

She must have left his office through another door as she didn't come past me.

'Been there long, Jane?' Michael asked, interrupting my thoughts.

I jumped, embarrassed. I realised from his casual stance he'd been watching me.

'Er, no. I just came in and thought I'd wait for you. I left my shopping in your office.'

'Oh, did you now?'

'Er, yes. Should I go and get it?'

'If you like,' he said, standing aside for me to pass him.

'Your friend, Mary, was just here,' he said.

'Oh, was she?' I said.

'Yes, she was, but I think you already know that, don't you?'

77

'What? Er, no… I don't… I don't know what you mean'

'Oh, I think you do,' he laughed. 'Perhaps its time for you to have a very special session yourself. What do you think?'

'Um, if you think it could help me, I suppose that would be good.'

'You look very sexy when you're lying, Jane,' he said coming closer to me. 'I'll bet your pussy's on fire.'

It was, but I wasn't going to tell him that.

'Lying! I'm… I'm not lying,' I said.

'Oh, I think you are,' he said. 'I think you already knew that Mary had been in here, didn't you?'

'Er, well,' I was never very good at not telling the truth.

'It's OK,' he said, as he grabbed the back of my head with one hand, pulling me forcefully into his body.

I tried to pull back, frightened by his strength, but he held me even tighter, breathing into my ear as he kissed my neck. I gasped when I felt his hand lift my skirt. He tore off my panties, leaving me breathless as the elastic left a stinging sensation.

'Please, don't,' I said half-heartedly.

'Hmm, that's not what your pussy's saying. I think you might enjoy a bit of a spanking too for spying on me.'

'I didn't. I didn't mean to. I think I should go now,' I said reluctantly as I felt a stirring deep inside me.

He pushed me back onto the couch and I tried desperately to fight him off. I didn't want to come across as too easy. He grabbed both of my hands and held them over my head, his other hand pushing my legs apart as he groped for his cock, rubbing my pussy with it before he quickly pushed inside me.

My body betrayed me by allowing his cock to slip in so easily. I felt myself responding and Michael looked down at me knowingly, a smile crossing his handsome face.

Bastard.

Still holding me firmly, he pushed deeper inside me, quickly bringing me to a wonderful orgasm. My eyes closed in ecstasy only to quickly fly open as I felt the sharp sting of pain as he slapped me hard on the thigh.

'Stop it!' I demanded, trying to struggle out of his grasp. 'Don't, Michael. I don't like it,' I said, as he slapped me again.

'Yes you do. Your pussy's getting really wet now. Oh, yeah, you like it all right. Come on, admit it?'

'I don't,' I pouted. I was enjoying it, but I didn't want Michael to know. Slapping me on the thigh with his open hand was one thing, but the thought of a whipping was definitely out of the question.

My pussy was on fire. With each slap, I felt myself building to a mind shattering orgasm. My juices flowed out of me, over his cock to dribble onto his balls. I couldn't stop. I was wild with desire.

'Oh, Michael,' I begged. 'Please don't stop. Don't stop.'

He laughed knowingly.

Letting go of my hands he rolled me over on top of him. I slipped in easily, impaling myself on him. I loved this position and began riding him, harder and harder, caressing my breasts as he held me firmly by the hips.

His hands encircled my waist and then slid down to my groin. His thumbs stroked downwards, massaging and opening my pussy lips wider, before rubbing my clit, teasing it as I bucked into him.

His hands were caressing my cheeks, pulling them apart as he gently ran his fingers around my hole, tickling it. I felt light slaps, in between caresses, getting harder and harder.

I could feel my pussy twitching as the stinging sensation of pain drove me out of my mind. My pussy wouldn't stop quivering. I was even more excited as I thought back to what he'd done to Mary, and the sheer pleasure I'd heard in her voice.

Finally, as we came together, I collapsed on top of him, my breathing erratic.

'Oh, God, Michael. That was fantastic.'

'I told you you'd enjoy it,' he said chuckling. 'Come on admit it?'

'Well, maybe just a little. But I don't want to do it again, OK?'

'Sure,' he said, stroking my hair. 'There's plenty more treatment I've got in store for you. I think we'll have to up your sessions now to three times a week, don't you?'

I could hardly wait, and to think I could claim it all on health insurance was an added bonus.

# Remembrance
## by Imogen Gray

My name is Elizabeth Warner-Jones and today I'm going to die. I am awaiting my fate in Newgate Prison having stood trial for the murder of my French lover, Sauville Chabrier. It is Valentines Day 1815. I sit in my high-waisted white muslin gown with a fashionable ribbon, white muslin cap and high-laced boots, it is my wedding outfit as I should be married today, instead I shall be hanged, hanged by the neck until I am dead. Is it really only three days ago the Recorder sentenced me? I recall being carried from the dock convulsed with agony and emitting frightful screams. I know my fate, I shall be led from my condemned cell into the Press Yard and my hands will be pinioned. It is a short walk to the scaffold, a Reverend will accompany me and ask if there is anything I need to communicate in my final moments and I will undoubtedly shake my head. If only he knew…

Sauville – I say his name out loud, allowing it to salivate from my lips sensuously. Sauville – the most magnificent man I have ever met, masculinity oozed from his every pore. We met quite surprisingly at the market place; he was very much the gentleman as he accidentally bumped into me, sending my shopping basket of fruit everywhere. Instead of ignoring me, dismissing me as a servant, he

81

proceeded to assist and replaced every last apple. I watched as his hands brushed the street grime from each one and placed them gently back into my basket. As my eyes met his he smiled brightly and I had foolishly fallen. His eyes, French accent, his charisma and ultimately his persuasive methods seduced me. It was not surprising that only three weeks later we would meet in Mrs Cooper's lodgings. He would pay beforehand, one afternoon's rental for the filthy room. Once a week I would meet my French lover, once a week I would experience desire, lust beyond my imagination and receive nine shillings.

Upon arrival he would pour me some wine, before I could sip it he would immediately begin to remove my clothes, tantalisingly slowly at first, whispering sweet kind words. 'You're beautiful, your skin is smooth as silk, I could stroke it for ever.' Then, like a sudden wave engulfing him, his eyes would darken, his lips would tighten and his touch would become firm, his fingers tightening around me, his arms forcing me downwards until I would be laid naked and shivering across his lap.

The first time he spanked me I screamed loudly but he placed his hand firmly across my mouth. 'Shhh' he said, 'it doesn't hurt really, more of a shock than anything.' I could taste the saltiness of sweat from his palms. I felt so utterly powerless in his grip, but amazingly excited. Within minutes his flat hand cracked downwards again upon my bare buttocks and I did not scream, I winced slightly but within seconds he would caress me, rubbing his hand so gently over the pert curve of my bare bottom. 'Poor little girl,' he would say, 'so red, so raw'. Occasionally he would bend down to kiss and nip at my bum cheeks. I would find myself relaxing to his touch, enjoying his fingers, smoothly, rhythmically, searching. His hand would continue to soothe and then a finger would gently intrude into me, I would utter a small sigh. 'You can feel that?' he would question.

82

'Oh yes' my back gently arching of its own accord as one, two fingers would encroach. He would hear me breathe louder and gasp.

'You're a bad girl Lizzie!' Then a sharp slap, so loud, like a clap of thunder. I would jump with fright but, so perceptive was Sauville, he would grasp me so firmly pushing me down into his lap, with my hair cascading around his legs, my hands touching the floor. 'Do not move my lovely, this will not take long,'

I knew I would not disobey, but occasionally the jolt of the spanks would move my body. Ten, maybe twelve, sharp slaps upon my bare buttocks, I would lose count. I would try not to cry but the pain would occasionally surge through my excitement and small tears would emerge.

If he detected a secret tear I would be berated. 'No tears, Lizzie, you are an evil wicked girl, I need to discipline you.' Only once I sobbed profusely, as his finger had caressed my anus, pushing deeper and deeper inside. The sensation had startled me at first and then I moaned with delight. It felt so forbidden, so sensual.

'More,' I asked, hoping he would push me beyond my limits. I imagined him entering me there, slowly easing his way into me. Angrily, he produced a small long piece of flat wood, coarse from being sawn. His spanking seemed exceptionally brutal.

'Extra special discipline for you, Lizzie,' he exclaimed, you have been so wickedly depraved.' But, as I lay across him, I could feel how hard he was. I managed to free my arm, raise it up to touch him and he groaned loudly like a wounded animal.

I pleaded with him, 'Take me like that, please.' I begged but he refused. Later, as he removed a splinter left from the wood he spanked me with, he seemed genuinely appalled by what he had done, kissing me gently.

But just before he left, the darkness in his eyes returned. Fully dressed, he threw me across the bed, pushing up my skirts, scraping at my petticoats to find my bare flesh. Once revealed he lavished extra spanks upon me whilst asking if I had learned my lesson. 'Yes, yes, I'm a good girl,' I reassured him. Unbuttoning himself he would be hard again.

'Take it, Lizzie,' as he forced himself into my mouth until he came. 'Swallow, Lizzie, drink me in,' he would demand.

As I walked home and felt the shillings in my palm, I wondered about him. Sauville, albeit immoral, had a hold over me. Did I hate the spanking, his discipline? No, I felt sometimes I did deserve it. I liked the things he did to me and perhaps that was wrong. But I knew he loved me, I was sure of it. Sometimes when he had dealt with my discipline he would make the tenderness of love to me.

Laying me down, kissing every inch of my body. Reassuring me that I was such a good girl now and I deserved a treat. We would stand together, him naked with his erect penis brushing gently against my tummy. Kissing me, his tongue entwining with mine, nipping at my lower lip. Gently he would push my shoulders down until my mouth was level and it seemed perfectly natural to take him gently into my mouth, gently licking, stroking him and listening to his contented breathing. As his breath quickened he would pull away, clasping me around my back and he would turn me around and lower my hands onto the edge of the bed.

I would be bent over for him to examine me. Again he would run his fingers over the red welts across my lower back and buttocks as if they were new to him. Shivering with pain and anticipation, I would wiggle, desperate for him to enter me.

Finally he would thrust deeply, forcing me forward, a hoarse growling sound emanating from his throat. His fingers firstly would pull my hair, my head lolling backwards, using it as a rein, as if he was riding me.

Thrusting, pushing harder and harder, until my knees felt they would buckle. Releasing my hair with one hand, his fingers would press between my legs, finding me, entering, twisting and caressing. His hands would then move forward clawing for my breasts, tweaking my nipples. Before he climaxed he would quickly withdraw, turn me around to lie flat on the bed. Straddling me, forcing my arms upwards and pinning them to the bed, he would push hard to enter me again. His eyes would be screwed tightly shut but mine were wide open, I could see the look on his face, how much he needed me, how much he loved me and I knew he would ask me to marry him. That is why I bought the dress, the nine shillings each week was saved and utilised wisely.

Mrs Cooper had been at Court. Her eyes looked evil and cat-like as she stared down at me. She would witness my hanging too. Mrs Cooper would feel it was her duty, being a vital witness. But then so would the Chemist's Clerk who kept the Poison Book. I had signed it just weeks before when I bought the arsenic to kill the rats. One signature for one glass bottle. The Clerk remembered my smile too, 'a happy lass, who would have thought it, about to commit murder.' How the arsenic had ended up in Sauville's wine bottle was surely down to me, they had established.

Mrs Cooper had explained that she knew Sauville was ill-treating me, she had heard my whimpers and cries through the walls of her lodgings as he had spanked me. Surely that was reason enough for me to poison him? Revenge, it had to be, they agreed.

And perhaps it was revenge but there was more.

More than the Court would ever hear, facts that I only I knew and would take to the grave. I had been spanked lightly that day, Sauville complained of feeling tired at first, but as I kissed and caressed him, he seemed to dance back to life.

'You want it, you sinful girl, don't you?' he shouted. I pulled up my skirts and bent over the bed for him, expecting to be spanked again. Without warning, his fingers jabbed straight into my anus. I yelled out in shock. 'Keep quiet, you've been wanting this,' he hissed. I tried to crawl forward but he hauled me back. Gripping my hair by the roots I felt trapped on all fours on the bed. I heard him releasing himself.

I panted loudly, half with fear, half with exhilaration. 'Not yet,' I pleaded weakly. Instantly his penis, hard and rigid, forced into my anus. I writhed a little on the bed but his grip did not loosen and I could feel myself excited and emitting juices down my legs. He let out a holler as he came and collapsed over me. As he stood and released me, I tried to lower my skirts but a sharp spank caught my buttock, I squealed with delight. 'You'll pay for that, Lizzie!' he snapped. Contentedly I smiled; I liked to please Sauville. As I left the lodgings he pressed the shillings into my hand and kissed my cheek. I decided then to broach with Sauville the subject of our marriage.

He laughed in my face. 'Lizzie, you deluded child, you're nothing but a plaything, a mere pastime to me. I have girls who venture far more into the depraved than you.'

The thought that others had been with my Sauville was too much to bear. They say that arsenic creates a burning sensation, much like my passion once blazed for Sauville.

The portable gallows are being used. I shall be led from my condemned cell into the Press Yard and then to the scaffold. I will proceed up the steps and then I shall see the crowd, thronging the streets, jostling for the best position to witness my demise. I wish for them to fall silent and I believe they will. They will be hoping to hear my prayers and my dying pleas. But I shall remain silent whilst the Reverend intones his. The white cotton nightcap will be placed over my head and then the noose. The pin will be withdrawn, releasing the trap; with the rope taut I will fall twelve inches to my death. My final thoughts will be of Sauville.

The rats still infest the pantry but Sauville can hunt no more.

# Spank Pants
## by Sommer Marsden

I saw them in the store. I was there to get pantry items and
dog food. All the boring stuff that makes the home
complete. I was not supposed to be buying clothes. Not. But
I needed new ones (I told myself) as I had lost a good
amount of weight. Working out, eating healthy, I *deserved*
them. And what better piece of clothing to buy than new
work-out pants. They were a necessity, just like the dry
goods and dog food. Plus, they were on clearance. How can
you pass up clearance work-out pants that are to die for?
That's easy. You can't.

Then I had a problem. I bought them. I loved them.
Should I wear them? I turned it over in my head after my
shower, while examining my new pants. They were a nice
shade of blue, meant to hug the tush and the curves. Both
my tush and my curves were looking spectacular these
days. They sat low on the hips, had a drawstring, and right
in the middle of the seat (right above the middle of my ass
crack) was a teeny tiny decorative flourish and a little skull.
Both girly and kick-ass. They were perfect.

I would wear them and I would hope that Grant wouldn't
notice. He's a guy. Guys do not notice new pants. Do they?

I put them on. I took them off. I did this several times.
Every time I put them on I would sneak a little peek in the
full length mirror. I would turn my ass to the glass and gaze

over my shoulder at my own bottom. My own bottom that looked (not to be conceited) ravishing in the pants. Then I would hear Grant in my head, *Not a penny, Marcy. Not one penny that you don't need to spend. Let's get our finances in order and then you can buy your shoes and your clothes and all that stuff. Promise me...*

And, dammit, I had promised. I had promised to keep wearing my baggy clothes until everything was in order. I climbed into my baggy yoga pants and looked. rubbish. You couldn't even see my ass. A potato sack would be more flattering.

Fuck it. I put them back on. This time I would stay in them. I would deal with Grant if need be.

An hour. It took an hour. What with the Military Channel, the crossword puzzle and the magazine that had come in the mail. I thought I was home free. Giddy with the fact that I had bought new sexy pants and he didn't notice. I was carrying my final load of laundry through the living room when it happened.

'Marcy?' That tone. I knew that tone. That was the oh-missy-you-are-in-trouble tone.

'Yes?' I kept moving. Maybe if I went upstairs he would forget.

'Come here, Marcy.'

Fuck.

'Why?' I tried to sound nonchalant. I tried to sound sure of myself. Defiant. I tried it all. What came out of my mouth was a high-pitched tone that basically screamed, *I'm sorry!*

'Please come here, Marcy.' He was smiling but, damn, I didn't trust him.

I set the basket at the bottom of he steps and went to him. Slowly. I hated feeling like a naughty little girl. All I had done was spent fifteen dollars on a pair of pants! The feeling was there nevertheless. I had lied. I had promised I wouldn't buy anything that was not a necessity and I had lied.

I stood in front of him and he took my hands in his. You would think with him seated on the sofa and me standing, I would feel a little less nervous. I would at least have the illusion of power. Wrong. It didn't matter that physically I was in the dominant position. I had guilt coursing through me like black poison and he knew it.

'I thought we made a deal.' He said it softly. Then he directed his stare at my gorgeous new pants.

'I–'

'Marcy?'

'Yes?'

'Are those new pants?'

'Well, they–'

'Marcy!'

'What!' I jumped at his harsh tone and my fluttery response. What the hell? Grant counted on me to do right but he was treating me like a child. To make matters worse, my body was responding to his tone in the most bizarre way. My nipples were hard and sensitive under my T-shirt and the crotch of my lovely new pants was…wet.

'Are those new pants?' He enunciated each and every word, letting them fall from his lips like heavy stones.

'Yes,' I sighed and hated myself for my grovelling tone. 'They were on clearance. They didn't cost much. I've worked so hard and I just wanted to have *one* pair of pants that actually fit. So I can see all my hard work,' I rushed on. I had to make him understand that it was only a small break in my promise. I really was on board with getting our finances straightened out.

'Turn around.'

'What?'

'You heard me. Turn around.'

It was the tone. That tone. A disciplinarian's tone. It transported me back to my Catholic school days and without thinking, I promptly turned my bottom to him and stood ruler straight.

*What are you doing!* My brain was protesting but my body was humming. I could feel little blips of excitement and dread and what could only be arousal pulsing under my skin. My cheeks were hot with shame and something else. I could feel my heart beating at the base of my throat, so hard it hurt a little.

He smoothed his hand over the skull that hid the treasure of my ass crack. I flinched a little even though it was a gentle touch. Something was coming. I could feel it. The air in our generic, homey living room felt thick and charged. It felt like the air before a violent thunder storm. I shivered and his hand smoothed lower, running over the firm underside of my left buttock.

'You made me a promise and you broke it,' he said softly. His hand roamed over to my right buttock and took a gentle tour of the soft fabric.

At first I thought the soft sound I heard was the sound of his work-callused hand on cotton. I realised when I heard the sound a second time, it was me. Sighing.

Grant placed his big hands on my hips and turned me. I went willingly. I had a quick mental flash of a ruler being brought down across my knuckles for writing on the white part of my saddle shoes in high school. I had been in Catholic school before they had outlawed the nuns doling out corporal punishment. This felt that way. I was about to be punished. Somehow the thought of being punished by my husband's large, warm hands made me squirm in my pretty blue pants.

As I faced him, he took my hands again and gazed up at me. The look on his face was both stern and sorrowful.

'You know how I feel about lying. I don't lie to you. You don't lie to me. That's been the deal. It always has been.'

I nodded. Part of me wanted to plead my case, remind him it was only a *little* money, apologise. A bigger part of me very much wanted what was coming to me. I remained silent.

'You broke your word to me, Marcy. Now I want you to lie across my lap.' He indicated his denim clad legs. He did not smile. There was no indication that this was a joke.

'I–'

'Now,' he said, quietly but there was clearly no room for argument.

My knees were shaking and my legs tingled. I positioned myself over his lap and fought the urge to raise a stink. This was ludicrous. It was insane. It was also clearly turning me on. The cotton crotch of my pants meant to absorb sweat was now flooded with my own moisture. A flutter had started low in my belly and my pulse was slamming so hard my ears were ringing.

I lay with my lower belly and pubic bone over his lap. My head hung down and the blood immediately rushed to it making me feel off balance. My legs dangled, my toes touching the floor.

'How much were the pants?' he asked. Finally!

'Fifteen dollars,' I said contritely.

'Fifteen it is,' Grant said. 'Count them off.'

Again the urge to climb off of him and give him hell surged through me. Again I let myself feel the growing urgency in my sex. In my breasts. Way up in the deepest part of me that made my belly feel achy and hollow. I nodded. I would count.

He smoothed his hand over my ass and when the hand withdrew I braced myself. Nothing. A moment when there was no contact and then his hands were caressing my

93

bottom again. Gentle. Lovingly. I relaxed into it, enjoying the sensation. Then too fast for me to register he brought his hand back and the first smack rang through the room.

'One,' I bellowed as my head shot up and the pain registered. Great coursing sizzles of heat ran through my flesh.

Another stroke and a second smack. This one a little harder than the first. He'd aimed to criss-cross the spot that was already flooded with heat and blood. 'Two,' I blurted and squirmed a little.

The pain had bled into the pleasure I felt and I was left with a confusing sensation of shame and arousal.

I sang out for each smack as it landed. Sometimes softer, sometimes harder. Each one ratcheted my pleasure up a notch. Each one made the heady feeling I had a little worse. When we hit ten a light sheen of sweat had broken out on my skin and I was gasping from pain and pleasure.

'Stand up,' Grant said.

'But that was only ten,' I protested. I damn well wanted my full punishment now.

'Stand up!'

I stood, resisting the urge to balk. He spun me roughly and yanked the drawstring nestled below my belly button. The pants loosened and slid to the floor with a soft sigh. Knickerless, ass singing with pain, I stood before him. This time when he turned me, it was slowly.

I held my breath. What now? Grant was keeping me off balance and that was both strange and amazing.

'You should see. Lovely. Every single one is gorgeous. All criss-crossed and red with little flecks of purple.' As his blunt fingers traced the imprints of his hands, I started to sag. His gentle touch on my tender skin was overwhelming and felt so good. I stood there and let him admire. He kissed along my right cheek first. His tongue hot and soothing on my skin. When he moved to my left cheek, I thought my legs might buckle and I would fall to the floor. Visions of his hard cock sliding into me filled my head.

I was not expecting it when he said, 'I think the final five should be on your bare bottom. It's only fitting, don't you think?'

First fear shot through me. My ass was already stinging and raw, now he wanted to spank my naked flesh? Then I felt another fresh rush of fluid between my thighs. That was it. My body had made the decision for me. I nodded.

He didn't even tell me to count but when the first blow fell I yipped, 'Eleven!'

'You should see what this well toned ass looks like when I hit it,' he whispered and then cracked me again before I could prepare.

'Twelve!'

Thirteen and fourteen had me at the point of dripping. My cunt was constricting impatiently against nothing, my nipples little painful nubs of desire. I felt his hot tongue dive the length of the seam of my ass and pushed back against him eagerly. Soothing. Hot. Warm. Wet.

*Crack!*

'Fifteen!' I sang and started to sag.

He caught me. Suddenly the disciplinarian was gone and my loving husband was back. He cradled me, lowered me to the sofa.

'Take off your jeans,' I pleaded.

'I'm halfway there, darling,' he laughed softly, popping the buttons one by one. I watched, transfixed as the little silver buttons parted to show me a pair of blue boxer briefs.

I wanted to reach out and shove them down and be aggressive the way I sometimes could be when we had sex, but I was too tired. I felt stripped and exhausted and raw. Used and abused, but in the most delicious manner.

I parted my thighs willingly, eager to have the length of him fill me. To make good use of the fluid and need my body had generated. He slid into me with one long stroke

95

and I felt the first flicker of orgasm from that single thrust. The flesh of my bottom burned, the pain coursed up my spine, making my scalp tingle and ache. But the pleasure he filled me with blended perfectly, accented the pain. Or the pain accented the pleasure. I wasn't sure. I didn't care.

Each thrust was heaven and I hung on tenaciously. I did not want to come yet. Not yet.

Grant watched my face, his face soft and sensitive again, then he pushed into me brutally hard, and barked, 'Come for me, Marcy.'

I obeyed. Unclenching my jaw and giving myself over to the intense stabs of pleasure that echoed through my body, I rode out the lovely, fluid waves of my orgasm as his tempo increased. A small sadness bloomed in my chest. I had wanted it to last longer. Once I came, Grant was always right behind me. My own release triggered his.

But not this time.

His face, once again dark and intense loomed over me. He fucked me roughly now. His movements a little frenzied, his breathing hard. He yanked my knees high and wide, leaned back to watch himself thrusting into me. I looked, too. Watched his long, rosy cock being swallowed by my body.

His eyes were on me again. Normally bright blue but now the colour of a storm over the ocean. 'I want you to come again,' he said, his thrusting so forceful I was being shoved against the sofa arm.

'I don't think I—'

He pounded into me and then pinched me. Hard. Right on the sore, recently abused flesh of my ass. I came. As Grant emptied into me I came long and hard for the second time, my body milking and working his cock.

When he collapsed on me, all the breath rushed from me. I couldn't breathe. The flickers of my orgasm were working through me like tiny strobe lights. Winking on and off throughout my body. My ass burned and hurt. I didn't care. I wrapped my arms and legs around his warm body and sighed.

'Bet you won't do that again,' he chuckled in my shoulder.

'Nope.' But the truth was, I was already picturing the other workout pants I had admired while shopping. Each and every pair on clearance. And, in my humble opinion, they were a necessity.

# My Husband's Idea
## by Eva Hore

'Come on, you'll love it' he whispered into my neck.

'No way,' I said.

I was preparing dinner. Michael had come up behind me with this mind-blowing proposition. I loved Michael and he loved me but I didn't want to do anything that could rock the boat.

'Why? Give me one good reason why you can't,' he insisted.

'Because…because I don't know…it just doesn't seem right,' I fumbled.

'What's the difference between how they see you at the beach and this?' he persisted.

'I'm wearing bikinis, for one thing.'

'Yeah, but most of the time you're topless. You still have your G-string bikini bottoms on and, let's face it, they don't leave much to the imagination do they?'

'Well, no, I suppose. I don't know,' I said, warming to the idea.

'What about that time we made love at the beach, in that cove? We both knew those guys were watching us. Remember how that turned you on?'

'Boy, do I? It was fabulous,' I grinned.

'It's the same sort of thing. Guys watching you. You know you're an exhibitionist. You'd love it. You've got the sexiest body, you know that. Guys are always checking you out.'

I smiled smugly to myself. It was very tempting.

'How would you feel?' I asked.

'I'd be wrapped. I know the guys are jealous of me, because I'm the one you're with. Come on Vanessa. It would give me so much pleasure to watch them squirm while you're stripping.'

'Really?' I giggled, putting the potato peeler down.

'You bet. Watching them watching you would be the biggest buzz for me. Knowing that when they go home to their frumpy wives and girlfriends, they'll be thinking of you,' he said.

That was it. That last line. Knowing they'd be thinking about me, and my body, while they're fucking their partners. That was what clinched it for me, but I didn't want Michael to think I was too keen.

'Well, I wouldn't know how to go about it,' I mused.

'It's easy. You just pick one good track and pretend you're stripping for me. Come on, let's practice now. Dinner can wait,' he said eagerly.

I stood there in the middle of the lounge while Michael flipped through his CDs. Michael certainly had a good idea. I wasn't shy about my body. In fact the more I thought about the more I wanted to do it. I thought back to that day at the beach. I'd never felt so turned on, knowing those guys were watching us. Secretly I wanted them to join in, but I never mentioned it to Michael. I didn't want him to think I wasn't happy with him or our lovemaking.

'I'll be back in a second,' I said, rushing out of the room.

In our bedroom I pulled the suitcase out from under the bed. Inside I had an assortment of costumes. I chose my schoolgirl outfit. It consisted of a short skirt, white underwear, white shirt, tie, short socks and runners. I quickly pulled off what I was wearing and took great pains to make sure I looked hot. I even put my hair in pigtails and returned to the lounge carrying some books.

Michael whistled his approval. Now I was excited to begin. He hit the play button and I began my agonising slow strip for him. First, I just sashayed around the room, giving him a glimpse of my white panties when I picked up the books I'd dropped, before flinging them on the couch beside him.

Then I tugged at my tie, slowly undoing it, inching it down to fling it over his neck and pull him close to my breasts, only to push him away when he tried to touch them. I left the tie hanging there, knowing I would use it again when it served my purpose.

I had the shirt loose over my skirt and as I undid each button, I watched Michael's reaction. He was licking his lips, sitting up straight, eager to see, eager to watch, so I dropped my shoulders back, shrugging, allowing the shirt to fall from my arms and onto the floor as I danced around the room.

The white push-up bra I was wearing looked fabulous against my tanned skin. We'd had a good summer and I had a tan you'd die for. My nipples were just poking over the tops and I ran a wet finger from my mouth, down my neck and into the cups. I squeezed my nipple, moaning as I did, my other hand travelling up my thigh and under my skirt.

'Come over here?' Michael pleaded.

'No,' I said.

'I said, come over here' he said more firmly.

'No.'

'Do you want me to spank you?' he asked.

'No.'

'Then do as you're told and come over here.'

I stood there before him, my breasts heaving as my breathing became more ragged. I had my hands clasped demurely in front of my skirt.

'Turn around,' he demanded.

101

I did.

'Bend over and let me see if you can touch your toes' he asked.

I did, feeling my skirt ride up high enough for him to see all of my panties. I felt his hands on my thighs as they roamed up towards my ass.

'Very nice,' he said, giving me a playful smack.

'Oh,' I said, girlishly flicking my hair back as I turned my head to look at him.

He was smirking and one hand was rubbing his crotch.

'You can turn back now,' he said.

'Please don't spank me,' I said. 'I'll be good. I promise.'

'I'm sure you will be,' he said. 'Now how about you drop that bra onto the floor?'

Un-clipping it from behind my back, I slipped the shoulder straps down and allowed my breasts to sway of their own accord. I knew how much Michael loved my breasts so I lifted them up in the palms of my hands and gently caressed them.

Pulling me towards him by my hips, he motioned for me to straddle him so he could smother his face into my cleavage. As his mouth sought out my nipples, I grabbed him by the back of the head and crushed him to me.

His erection was throbbing against me. I squirmed in his lap, enjoying his discomfort. His tongue licked crazily at my nipple before he sucked it into his mouth, biting down gently on the nipple, pulling back, stretching it out until I cried out.

'That didn't hurt,' he said.

'Yes, it did,' I pouted.

'Are you disagreeing with me?' he asked.

'It's my nipple. I think I know when it's hurting or not,' I teased, knowing he was itching to give me a spanking.

'Stand at once. I don't like disobedient girls,' he said, giving me a slap on the thigh.

'Bend over my knee,' he demanded.

'No,' I said.

'Don't disobey me again,' he said, and then more firmly. 'Bend over my knee.'

I did and balanced myself with my arse pointing deliciously upward. His fingers pulled my skirt up to the back of my waist and then he inched my panties down just enough to expose the cheeks.

'Hmm,' he said, 'you have a nice arse, a really nice arse.'

I giggled as he ran his hands over my cheeks in circular motions, enjoying the light slaps he was giving me.

'You like me spanking you, don't you?' he asked.

'No,' I said. 'I don't.'

'I think you do. Let me see,' he said, pulling my panties further down so they were at the back of my knees. 'Oh, yeah, I can see your pussy and it's glistening. You do like me spanking you, don't you?'

I didn't answer, enjoying this game. So much for the stripping, I thought, as his finger slipped down my crack and into my wet pussy. I opened my legs a fraction as he located my clit and smeared it with my juices.

Suddenly something hard smacked into my right cheek, stinging me. Wow, what the hell was that? I peered over my shoulder and saw he had a schoolbook in his other hand and was raising it up high to smack me with it again.

'Ow,' I complained. 'That hurt!'

He kept on doing it while his finger slipped further into my pussy. My hands were resting on the floor and I held myself rigid. My cheeks were becoming numb but my pussy was alive. Very alive and wanting much more attention. Finally he stopped.

'Stand up,' he commanded.

My panties were still at my knees and as I stood I stumbled. He grabbed me firmly by the hips, his fingers unzipping the skirt. It dropped to the floor with my panties and I kicked them off my feet.

103

I stood there naked before him in only my white socks and runners. He turned me around, kissing my cheeks and then his tongue soothed my skin as he licked over the welts. His fingers opened up the cheeks and his tongue slipped down over my hole.

'That's one hot arse,' he said. 'Now I want you to lean over the edge of the couch. I want your arse pointing up and your legs spread. Do you think you can do that without complaining?'

'Yes,' I said, moving into position.

'I'll be back in a minute. Don't move an inch,' he said.

I stayed there like that for probably five minutes, wondering what he was up to. He returned and stood there, casually patting my behind. Then his hand cupped my pussy, squeezing it a bit, one finger slipping inside.

'Very nice,' he said. 'Very nice,' then slapped me hard on the pussy.

I wasn't expecting that and I cried out. He ignored me and I felt the hard smack of his hand, again and again. Blood coursed through my body and I knew my pussy was becoming engorged with blood. It began to throb maddeningly.

'Don't turn around,' he commanded.

He stood back and I saw from the corner of my eye that he was removing his clothing, dropping his trousers and briefs in one go and stepping out of them. I heard the rustle of clothing and sensed his shirt had been removed as well.

He stood behind me and his knob roamed around my derriere, then the tip of it was nudging my pussy. I opened my legs wider, pointing my buttocks up higher, wanting him to fuck me. He slapped me hard on the thigh as his knob continued to probe at me, inching in a fraction and then pulling back. He did this for a while and I knew what was coming next.

He was lubricating his knob with my silky juices so he could enter my hole. We didn't do this much, only on special occasions and I guessed this was to be one of them. Michael's fingers were probing around my hole, opening my cheeks, as his knob slipped further upwards.

Very slowly he began to inch it in, massaging my cheeks as he went. It slipped in easily and he grabbed my hips and brought me back towards him. I lifted myself up so I was resting on my hands. This allowed his cock to slip in further and when he began to pump, my pussy throbbed in time.

I moved one of my hands down and located my throbbing clit. It was hard and ready for a rub. I teased it out from under the hood, flicking it with my fingers before focusing on the very centre of it, enjoying my finger as it caressed it lovingly.

Michael was fucking my rear end and every now and again he'd give one of the cheeks a slap. He was turning me on like never before and I rubbed my clit faster, thrilling at the sensation. My pussy was contracting, gapping open, wanting to be filled with his cock.

Suddenly something hard was pushing in. Something hard and cold. Whatever it was, it was big. I adjusted my position accordingly as it slipped further in. My pussy was so hot that when he pulled it back out, the coldness had all but disappeared.

As Michael fucked and pushed this foreign object in, I rubbed my clit madly and came. Michael fucked faster, holding me firmly by my hips now, allowing whatever had been in my pussy to fall out. He pumped in and out, my breasts swaying under the force of his thrusting.

Balanced over the armrest as I was, I pushed back into Michael and heard him cry out. He kept pumping releasing every drop into me as he gripped my hips tighter, his fingers digging into my flesh. I could feel droplets of sweat falling onto my back as he slowed down and finally pulled out. His come dribbled down my legs as I rolled from the couch and collapsed onto the floor.

He was on his knees trying to catch his breath, so I crawled over to him, taking his cock into my mouth, sucking on it as I massaged his balls. In no time his cock was hard, his balls full, ready to go again.

'You are so fucking sexy,' he said, looking down at me as I gobbled his cock.

My eyes smiled back at him as his hand slipped down my body and into my pussy. I loved being this wet. He knew how much I loved him fucking me and even though I liked it up the rear, I couldn't go past his cock in my pussy. He was the best fuck. I couldn't get enough of him.

'Whoa,' he said, his hands holding my head, pulling me away.

'I hope this makes you see how difficult it would be for me to strip around you?' I said. 'We can't keep our hands off each other.'

'I know,' he said. 'But I do have another idea.'

'Oh,' I said. 'What is it this time?'

'What about our own movies?'

'What?'

'You know,' he said. 'We could make our own pornos and hire them out? You always said you'd like to have an audience? Well, now you can. We could dress you up in all sorts of costumes. Tie you up to the bed, spread-eagled at my mercy. Fuck in the spa, with bubbles cascading over your gorgeous breasts. Lay you out on the table covered in fruit. Remember when we did that? You loved it. Eating the food right off you. Yeah, we could do so many different movies. We could set up nights right here at home.'

I was still on the floor, naked with just the socks and runners. My mind was in a spin. How did I feel about it? Well, just talking about it had my pussy throbbing. Watching guys watching me would certainly be a turn on for me.

'I don't know,' I said.

'It would be great,' he said. 'We could act out every fantasy you've ever had. Imagine, if we charged £20 a movie. We could easily fit 10 guys in here. Once they've seen the first movie, they'd want to see more. At £20 a time, we could realistically make enough money for a deposit on our own home in a few months. What do you think?'

'I don't think you should tell the guys it's me, you know, pretend it's someone else?' I said, my mind running along with the idea.

'No, that's silly. They'd know it was you.'

'Do you really think they'd go for it?' I asked.

'I'm sure they would. If we do this and you like it, maybe, for some extra cash, you could come in and strip as well. You know, if you feel more comfortable about it by then. We could make a fortune. What do you think?'

'I think you'd better come over here and fuck me,' I said, opening my legs as I lay back on the floor.

In a flash he was between them. 'You horny bitch. Everyone should be able to see what you've got. Let them fantasise about you. I'd be the only one fucking you. They're only allowed to watch.'

'Oh, fuck me harder, baby,' I said, on the brink of a powerful orgasm.

Yes, the thought of me being able to watch them watching me and maybe even come out when they're all hard, strip in front of them while they rub their cocks, yeah, that would be great. The more I thought about it the hornier I got. I bucked back into Michael wanting to be fucked harder.

'Oh, God, yeah, baby. Fuck me,' Michael yelled. 'Let's show the world what a great fuck you are. Oh, yeah, I'm coming,' he breathed into me ear.

Just thinking about it had me hotter than ever before. I couldn't wait to begin taping. I was even thinking about having some of them there while we taped. Maybe I could

107

suck someone's cock while Michael fucked me. I wondered if he'd go for it.

Then the most powerful of orgasms rocked me. I exploded in a rush of juices, frantically punching Michael's back. We lay together spent, exhausted. This was a brilliant idea of Michael's. We could make a fortune. Be in our own home, make movies, maybe even sell them. And if I could involve other guys to spice up the movies, Michael would have to agree and I'd have the best of both worlds.

In less than a few hours I'd gone from a hesitant participator to a raving nympho. I couldn't wait to get started. I looked over towards the couch and saw a courgette lying on the floor. Obviously the foreign object Michael had fucked me with earlier.

The image was vivid; lying on a table, covered in fruit with guys eating from my body, their mouths touching every part of me, their tongues licking, their fingers feeling; each of them taking a bite out of say, a banana, from my pussy. Their mouths, lips and tongues all tantalising me as they took it in turns to nibble off it. Oh, yeah. I was getting wetter by the second.

Michael was an ideas man and I had to admit that this idea was his best one yet.

Look out for us; we'll be out there soon. I'm the one with the real tits, the real smile and the real orgasms. I'll be the one having all the fun.

# Wanton Witchery
## by Lynn Lake

Bridgette struggled against the coarse rope that bound her thin wrists, pulled her aching arms up over her head. The rope ran up and through a pulley fastened into the ceiling, and then down into the hands of one of the monks. He had only to tug on the hemp to jerk Bridgette's slender, stretched arms even higher above her head. He tugged on it many times.

The hoist was just one of a multitude of pain-inducing devices that the two brown-robed Dominican monks had at their disposal to ferret out witchery. Scattered about the dingy, cobwebbed dungeon were other, vastly more terrible, instruments of the Inquisition – whips and chains and paddles, thumbscrews, manglers, a nail-studded chair, and hanging ominously from the ceiling: the iron gate, a four-by-six-foot bed of razor-sharp pikes fastened to a heavy, cast-iron frame, suitable for eviscerating any poor innocent tied to the rack.

Bridgette's long, shimmering, brown tresses hung about her pale face and shoulders, her virginal white summer dress torn to ribbons by the monks. Her soulful, brown eyes dripped tears, as brackish water in turn dripped down upon her face from the rotted ceiling of the crypt-like chamber which lay at the fetid bottom of the monastery. Her heavy breasts jerked up and down in rhythm to her ragged breathing.

The monks, their faces shrouded in the darkness of their woollen hoods, slavered with delight as they gazed upon Bridgette's heaving chest, jutting, kitten-pink nipples riding damp, undulating breasts. They stared at the girl's downy-furred sex as well, licking their bloodless lips.

The taller of the two monks shuffled over to a wooden bench, picked up a studded, round, wooden paddle, and shuffled in behind the hanging girl. 'Let the power of Almighty God beat the Devil out of the possessed soul of this wanton!' he cried, smashing the paddle across Bridgette's plush, plump buttocks.

Her body jerked, the pulley groaning. Her luminous eyes glazed and her full-bodied lips trembled, as the wooden paddle cracked against the gleaming orbs of her mounded butt cheeks again and again and again.

The monks brayed with laughter, their sharp teeth showing white in the black holes of their hoods. The paddle came up, crashed down on the ample, jiggling flesh of Bridgette's ass, striking her over and over, smooth, porcelain skin flushing violently scarlet, her bottom absorbing the savage blows and sending them vibrating all through her dewy body.

The monk holding the rope quivered as Bridgette quivered, as his merciless companion relentlessly smacked the paddle across the girl's ripe ass. 'God have mercy!' she wailed, desperately tilting her head heavenward as the monk paddled hellishly on.

'My turn, brother!' the shorter monk finally rasped, after Bridgette's bountiful bottom had been thoroughly singed by the singing paddle. He tossed his compatriot the rope that stretched Bridgette upright and scurried over to the bench, grabbing up a leather horse-whip, briefly testing its strength and flexibility with his trembling fingers. Satisfied, he hurried back in behind the girl, hissing, 'Turn the other cheek, slut of Satan!'

Eyes gleaming from within the murk of his cowl, he raised the whip over his head and then brought it whistling down on Bridgette's battered rear end. The crack of vicious impact was only slightly louder than the ragged scream that tore loose from Bridgette's parched throat and echoed throughout the dungeon.

'Beat her, brother!' the other monk shrilled. 'Beat the word of God into the immoral wench!'

The monk with the whip slashed at Bridgette's provocative cheeks over and over, his breath thundering out of his nose and mouth. She writhed around on the end of the rope, outstretched toes barely scraping the stone floor. Her trembling buttocks blazed red as a fiery sunset, then a deeper purple, hard white ridges forming on the blistered flesh where the sting of the whip was harshest.

'Enough!' the taller monk wheezed, loosening his grip on the rope. The pulley creaked and the ravaged lovely collapsed in a pool of wetness on the cold floor.

He roughly grabbed Bridgette's silky locks and yanked her head back, tore away the tattered remnants of her youthful dress. The other monk stood and stared, lungs bellowing, whip still jerking in his skeletal hand. He finally dropped the flesh-biter and assisted his brother in dragging the moaning girl over to the bench, draping her over the top of it.

The two emissaries of the Old Testament eyed Bridgette's swollen, welted buttocks, and then each other. The paddler proved quicker, hiking up his sacred robe to reveal a twitching, blood-engorged erection. 'It is time for this Devil's whore to be penetrated by the righteous lances of Christian soldiers!' he exclaimed.

The whipper eagerly nodded. He grasped Bridgette's flayed, overfull butt cheeks and spread them wide, opening her up to the sword of God. His blunt fingernails bit into her tenderised flesh, and she groaned, clawed splinters out of the crude bench.

111

The taller monk spat into his hand and rubbed his rigid cock with the hot saliva, swirling his bony fingers up and down his veiny length. The monk holding Bridgette's ass open spat into her gaping crack, coating her pink, puckered anus with his own saliva. He inched a dirty finger closer to her exposed opening, then plunged it inside, violating the shrieking girl.

The monk brutally twisted his finger around inside Bridgette's bum, and she bit her lip, her legs shaking out-of-control as all shake before the might and majesty of the Inquisitors. 'Make way for the iron will of God!' the taller monk cried, driving his slimy, bloated hood into the raw, red hole which his brother had just vacated.

Karl was closing the barn door, after checking up on his livestock in prelude to turning in for the night, when his friend, Josef, came dashing down the dusty lane that tied his humble hut to the road.

'Karl! Karl!' Josef yelled.

Karl ran out to meet Josef, halting the panting young man in his tracks by firmly grasping his shoulders. 'What is it, Josef?' he asked, as his friend fought to regain his breath.

'D-did Bridgette… go to the monastery tonight?' Josef finally gasped, his frightened eyes searching Karl's.

Karl nodded. 'Yes. She had some sewing to take to the brothers. She often mends their vestments.'

'Oh, merciful God!' Josef wailed, staring blindly up at the starlit heavens. 'I-I was in the monastery just now – bringing the monks some meat they had purchased from me – and I heard… I heard…'

'What did you hear!?' Karl demanded, roughly shaking his friend.

'I heard… screams coming from the cellar – where the Inquisitors do their wretched work!'

Karl's massive, muscular body went rigid. 'Bridgette!?' he hissed through clenched teeth.

112

'I-I think so! Yes, I think it was the voice of your betrothed...'

Karl swept Josef aside with one of his tree-trunk arms, his sky-blue eyes gone cold and bleak as winter, giant hands clenching into battering-ram fists. He raised up his mighty arms and bellowed, 'Nooo!'

Ever since the papal bull against witches had been unleashed in 1484, a savage wave of brutality and misery had engulfed the Low countries, sweeping up wrongly-accused young women in its crimson tide, leaving their battered bodies in its bloody wake. And now the terrible fanaticism had claimed Karl's beloved, whom he well-knew to be no witch.

Muscled arms pumping and powerful legs churning, he set off down the lane, racing out into the moonlit road for the monastery that lay a mere two miles beyond. His soul could be damned to the everlasting fires of Hell and back, for all he cared, before he'd let any Inquisitor torture a false confession out of his fiancée.


The monk ruthlessly penetrated Bridgette's asshole with his cock, shoved recklessly forward, sinking hard, unyielding meat deep inside the whimpering girl. And when his balls bounced against her ravaged butt mounds, and he was fully-buried in her hot, tight hole, his crooked mouth dropped open in exultation.

He moved his hips, slowly at first, surging his heavy cock back and forth in Bridgette's gripping chute. His brother beat her shuddering cheeks in time to the thrusting, handprints showing white on the seared flesh and then fading, and then not fading at all, as the fucking went faster, the blows raining down quicker. The one monk pounded Bridgette's ass with his cock, the other with his hands, sweat pouring from their cowls down upon the blasted flesh of the assaulted girl.

Faster and faster they went, harder and harder, the obscenely wet splashing of heated flesh against heated flesh filling the mouldering chamber. 'Let the scalding truth of your sins reveal themselves!' the fucking monk howled, rocking the girl with his cock, splitting her in two.

Bridgette moaned, screamed, banged her fists on the wooden bench, one monk pumping and one monk smacking her butt, the both of them, the all of them, in a frenzy now. The fucking monk grunted, gasped, his flapping balls boiling out-of-control and blazing white-hot fire into Bridgette's being. He jerked with the wicked intensity of his savage orgasm, the girl's sucking ass draining his spurting cock.

'Fill her with the cleansing seed of the Lord!' the other monk wailed, before sinking his teeth into the bountiful flesh of Bridgette's shivering buttocks.

The taller monk pulled out of Bridgette with a pop, and staggered backwards, empty, his cock flopping its uselessness. He grabbed onto the cruel iron gate for support, slicing open a finger on one of its sharp lances. His companion quickly yanked his own robe up and steered his iron rod into the gaping opening between Bridgette's blistered ass cheeks.

Then, all of a sudden, the cellar door burst open, was smashed clear off its hinges, and Karl stumbled into the sunken, dank chamber. He gazed in horror at his beloved bent over the bench, her buttocks flaming, the obscenely-engorged cock of a monk oozing inside her. 'Step away from her, you unholy bastards!' he roared at the stunned disciples.

They stared at the sweat-soaked colossus, watching in awe as he rushed forward. Karl seized the shorter monk by the back of the neck and jerked him out of Bridgette's ass, preparatory to flinging him against the ancient stone wall and splitting his head open.

114

He would have done so, but was arrested by the frantic voice of his fiancée.

'No, Karl!' she shrieked, twisting her head around. 'This is how I want it! This is why I come here!'

He froze. One look at her and he knew he would spare the depraved monk's life. Bridgette's desperate, indecent words sunk like lead into his fevered brain. He gazed into her shining, brown eyes. He smelled the musky scent of her dripping cunt assailing his flared nostrils, her burning bottom still undulating with the aftershocks of her orgasm.

Now he knew why she was the way she was. He now knew the mystery of the unnamed illnesses that always followed her visits to the monastery and kept her hidden from him for days afterwards. Now it all began to make some sort of sick sense.

'This is how I want it!' Bridgette shrieked again, dark, ravenous, orgiastic lust contorting her angelic face.

# Gym Shoe
## by Ivana Chopski

Janine bit her bottom lip in anticipation of what was about to happen, she bit so hard she felt a tooth pierce the skin. She could taste that unmistakable metallic tang on her tongue at the same time that she felt the warm liquid slowly run over her lip and head towards her chin. She wiped the blood away with the back of her hand, she didn't want him to see it, he might stop and it had been hard enough getting this far!

Today was Monday, not just any Monday because today was her fortieth birthday. They, her and her husband Ricky, had been out on Friday night for a celebratory meal. He'd taken her to the Greek place she loved in the High Street. She'd had the lamb, she always had the lamb and they had managed to polish off two bottles of Retsina, probably half a bottle too much, and then they had Ouzo with the coffee. Not a good move!

Ricky had moved from around the table where he was sitting opposite her and tucked himself next to her when the coffee arrived. He kissed her on the cheek and held her hand.

'Is there anything special you want for your birthday? I have got you something, but this is the big four zero and if there is something you've been longing for perhaps there's still time for me to sort it out,' he said without taking a breath, in a drink-induced slur.

Janine had pulled him close and, without thinking, whispered 'Spank me!'

Ricky couldn't have heard her right because he replied, 'Hankies? that's not a very good present and anyway you have loads of hankies!'

She tried again.

'Fuck off! You're kidding me!' Ricky said in disbelief, a tad too loud, as half the restaurant turned around to see what was going on.

'Shhhhhh!' she hissed at him.

'You want me to slap your arse?'

'No!' she said trying to keep her composure, lowering her voice to a whisper to stop the people on the table behind eavesdropping.

'No, I want to dress up as a schoolgirl; you catch me being naughty, then put me over your knee and spank me with a gym shoe!'

'Where...' he started and realised he was being loud again and in a whisper finished '...did this all come from?'

'I dunno; just thought it would be a bit of fun, spice things up a bit. You know?'

She had lied! She didn't like lying to him and did it very rarely but she couldn't tell him the real reason. She'd kept this secret to herself for twenty-four years, twenty-one of which she had been married to Ricky, and there was no way she was telling him, or anyone, now!

She was sixteen years old and a pupil at an all-girl Catholic school when it happened. It was a very strict environment to grow up in and Janine didn't always toe the line. One day in a physical education lesson she wouldn't take her turn on the trampoline, she was frightened but wouldn't admit as much. When the nuns tried to force her on it she wet her pants. They thought she had done it on purpose and had called for one of the priests to discipline her.

He had told her off and had asked her to apologise to the class, she had been unrepentant, protesting it was an accident. So he pulled a gym shoe out of his back pocket and positioned a chair in front of the whole class. They all sat and watched as he bent her over his knee and pulled down her gym shorts to reveal her bare backside. Then without warning he brought the shoe down hard on her white plump flesh. She had shouted out, in surprise more than pain, it had hurt or maybe stung but not a lot and by the time the third stroke landed it was more of a pleasure than a pain! She had noticed her nipples starting to harden, her clitoris throb and, by the sixth and final time, she was close to orgasm. Being spanked in public had brought out the exhibitionist in her – or would have done – if the opportunity had ever arisen.

It had been her guilty secret all that time, she had wanted to replicate the pleasure but was afraid to ask. Now she'd asked and he was looking at her like she'd gone completely mad!

'You bored with our lovemaking?' His voice brought her back to the present.

'No!'

'What then?'

'Oh, nothing, I wish I had never mentioned it!'

The waiter had arrived with the bill at that point and the topic wasn't mentioned again. Janine thought Ricky had forgotten all about it as he was a bit worse for wear with the alcohol; it wasn't until her birthday that she realised he hadn't!

They had both taken the day off work but had got up as usual, so the kids could give their mum her present and sing 'happy birthday' before they went off to school. When they were both alone in the house, Ricky brought out another present he'd been hiding under the stairs. It was quite a

119

large box wrapped in birthday paper with a huge bow on the top.

'What's this?'

'A special birthday surprise, hope you like it!' he said with a wink.

Janine placed it on the table, opened it up and placed the contents next to the box. There was a pale blue polo shirt, a short pleated skirt, a pair of white cotton panties, a pair of white knee-high socks, a pair of white rubber gym shoes and one larger black gym shoe. He looked at her with a wry smile and she blushed.

'I thought you forgot.'

'No way, this is what you wanted for your fortieth and this is what you are getting! Go upstairs and get changed.'

She had gathered up all her bits and gone to get changed. He had changed into his best suit by the time she came downstairs and was holding the black shoe, slapping it into his hand in a menacing manner. She had tied her hair into bunches, put on some make-up and felt like a schoolgirl again.

Ricky looked at her as she walked down the stairs and fell in lust with her all over again. She looked fucking hot! She always looked good, he thought to himself, she was tall, curves in all the right places with great legs and she carried this look very well. As if she knew what he was thinking, and she probably did, she started to accentuate the way she swung her hips as she cleared the last few steps, flicking her skirt to show a brief glimpse of her underwear.

Ricky moved forward and wrapped his arms around her, feeling his way up her skirt and down her pants, cupping the cheeks of her arse in his large hands. They kissed, a long lingering kiss, their tongues exploring each other's mouths as if they had never kissed before. Janine knew he was consumed because she was wearing that cherry lip gloss he hated the taste of and he hadn't wiped it off! She stopped kissing him and pulled away.

120

'Is that any way for a teacher to treat his pupil?'

He looked at her dejectedly like a scolded puppy and wiped the back of his hand over his mouth ridding himself of the cherry poison!

'What now?' he said grumpily.

'You tell me off, put me over your knee and spank me.'

'How many times, how hard, how will I know if I'm hurting you?'

'Slow down! Six times I think and you'll know how hard when it comes to it, I'm sure. Don't do it too soft though or it won't be worth it! We'll have a code so you know if I want you to stop.'

'What?'

'Well, if I shout out OW! Or Stop! I might not really mean it and will still want you to carry on so we need a word like, like 'monkey' which will mean stop.'

'Monkey?'

'Yes monkey, but only stop if I say monkey!'

'Have you done this before?'

'No! I watched a program on television and they talked all about this stuff.'

'Ok if you're sure, what now?'

'Tell me off!'

'What did you do?'

Janine let out a long sigh, thought for a moment then wet her pants.

'Janine, what the fuck! that's going to be great on my good suit!'

She frowned at him.

'Oh yeah, sorry!' and raising his voice, 'what have you done young lady?'

'Sorry, sir, I pissed my pants!'

'You know the punishment for that, don't you?'

She nodded, shamefaced, trying not to smile.

'You can wipe that smile off your face!' Ricky snapped starting to revel in his role.

121

'Bring me my slipper!'

She brought the slipper to him as he was moving a chair into the centre of the room. He sat on it and barked 'over my knee!'

Ricky wasn't sure exactly how he felt at that moment, a combination of feelings was coursing through his body, fighting each other for supremacy. He was worried about hurting her but he loved her and wanted to give her what she wanted, even if it was all a bit alien to him. The overriding feeling at the moment, though, was that of guilt, guilt because he was about to spank his wife and guilt because he hadn't felt this horny in years! What did they say about there being a fine defining line between pain and passion? He could see some sense in that if he thought about it. Say someone walked up to him and pinched his nipple; that would hurt him but if she was to bite his nipple while making love, that was horny! Maybe that was what this was all about, passion and pain? Well he was just about to find out.

Janine lay over his knee resting the palms of her hands on the floor, she could feel his cock pressing against her stomach and it was rock hard. The fact that this was arousing him started to turn her on. He flipped her skirt up onto her back to expose her panties, which he pulled down to reveal her white rounded bottom. He stroked it gently and as he did so she felt him getting harder, if that was possible. He picked up the slipper and her heart was racing.

The anticipation was really intense now and she was starting to get worried, what if it wasn't how she remembered? All this time fantasising, reliving, wanting something that could never be replicated, or, was never that good in the first place! What if it had been nothing to do with the spanking and had just been some exhibitionist trip, getting off on everybody seeing her bare arse?

'OWWW!'

122

Ricky had brought the slipper down on her bare backside, it hadn't been that hard but she wasn't ready for it. He must have realised as the next one was harder, it stung, stung in a good way! The old feelings were coming back! Again, harder still, she was holding back the tears as she felt her clit throb and her nipples harden. Was she crying because it hurt, or because of a realisation that she had remembered it right for all those years? Whack, whack, each one slightly harder than the last, the final one stung like fury!

After he spanked Janine for the sixth time, Ricky threw the gym shoe on the floor, grabbed her, pulled her to her feet and, holding her face with both of his hands, kissed her with a passion they hadn't felt for years.

He looked into her bright blue eyes and could see a longing and a desire that stirred his soul. As he wiped away a tear that had formed in the corner of her eye, time seemed to stand still. In that moment his senses were accentuated, he could feel her warm breath on his face, smell the conditioner in her hair and the subtleness of her perfume on her neck. In his temples was the beat of his, or her, heart, maybe both?

Without letting her go, he walked her backwards to the dining room table, managed in a seamless move to lift her to a sitting position on the table and unbutton his trousers. He opened her legs, slipped her panties to one side of her very moist pussy and, dropping his boxers to his ankles, entered her. They were both close to climax but they fucked with an intensity like nothing they had ever felt. When they finally came, Janine lay back on the table and he fell on top of her. They held each other tightly for what seemed like an eternity, with his cock still throbbing inside her.

Janine reached up so she could whisper in his ear.

'You like?'

'I like!'

'Guess what I want for Christmas?'

# The Landlady
## by Primula Bond

'I've come about the room.'

I look at the pretty girl hovering on the doorstep and find myself crossing my arms, just like a cartoon landlady.

'I thought with a name like Robin that you'd be a boy.'

The girl blushes all the way from her throat to her freckled cheekbones. She shifts her backpack about. I can see her breasts jiggle under her pink vest.

'You'd rather have a boy, Mrs Mason?'

'Wouldn't we all, Robin.' I can't help smiling. She takes that as an invitation to walk into my hallway, dark after the brilliant sunshine. 'Oh, wouldn't we all?'

But she doesn't smile back. Her shoulders slump. The backpack slides off, thumps to the floor.

'You OK, love? Want some water or something? It's a bloody heat-wave out there.'

She nods, glances up the stairs. 'I'm just tired, Mrs Mason.'

'Linda.'

'I had to leave my other place in a hurry, you see. So could I just see the room?'

I push her gently ahead of me, and follow her up the stairs. I've rejected all the other females. I want a hunky lad, his first time away from home, perhaps needing some TLC. Male company for me. I've fantasised about our little life, about casually leaving my bedroom door open, letting him see me naked. I'm in very good shape. What red-blooded male doesn't lust after big tits and juicy hips to grab? Forty might seem old to him, but I'd show him how good an older woman can be. Maybe I'd share wine with him one night, let him talk, maybe about his mum. I'd say things to heat him up. Make him forget all about his mum. I'd watch him go up to bed, then follow, tiptoe into his room, push aside the duvet, spread myself over him, slide onto his young, stiff prick before he can stop me. Oh yes. Make him feel *really* at home.

I certainly don't want to find myself mothering some bra-less waif with a long red plait and, admittedly, I now notice, very cute buttocks twitching in those cut-off shorts.

'So what went wrong?' I ask, showing her into the bedroom. 'Was your last landlady horrible to you?'

Robin wriggles on to the bed and blushes again. 'Landlord. Yes and no.'

I sit down beside her. 'Go on.'

'He tied me up.'

'That's terrible! He kept you prisoner?' I bite down on my lip, tasting blood. I find myself staring at the girl's breasts, straining at her vest, and my own nipples go hard. 'Should we call the police?'

'Not prisoner, exactly. I mean, I was free to come and go.' Robin shrugs, leans down to rub her thighs. Suddenly she's the cool one, and I'm hot and bothered. 'It was only at night, when I got home.' Robin glances up at me. Her blue eyes are glittering.

'You poor love.' I grip the edge of the bed. My stomach draws tight. 'Tell me everything.'

'It just happened one evening. He was putting up some shelves in my room. I lay on my bed. I was knackered after work.'

'Like you're tired now?'

126

She leans back, pulling her legs up. Our arms brush. 'I must have drifted off, because when I opened my eyes again my wrists were tied together, just like this –' she joins her hands and lifts them in the air. Her pert tits lift up, too. 'And the odd thing was, it was kind of – relaxing. Knowing I couldn't do anything. He was standing at the end of the bed, stroking the inside of my leg.' She lowers her arms, and stares straight into my eyes. 'I know I should have been scared, Linda. But it was turning me on. And he said it was only a game.'

The use of my name makes us feel close. I put my hand on her arm, and start to stroke it. But I feel anything but motherly. Her skin is soft, and warm, with golden hairs glistening under my fingertips. There's a strip of brown belly between her vest and the button of her shorts. 'For it to be a game, Robin, you have to enjoy it.'

Robin nods. She leans towards me so that we're nearly nose to nose. Her tits poke through her vest, dangle down. She crosses her legs Buddha-style, and her shorts dig right into her crotch, outlining the crack. I stare at it. Fine if it was a boy's crotch. You can stare them into an erection, but I've never stared like this at a girl's cunt. I am imagining the puffy lips under there, probably waxed and totally bare. A little slick of dampness over the soft skin, maybe, from walking through this heat. From sitting close to me on this bed.

'That's just it, Linda,' she whispers, glancing down to where I'm looking. She wriggles slightly, parting her legs even more. Is that a very faint whiff of female scent? My heart starts thumping. She smiles again. We're so close I can hear the moisture as she stretches her mouth, licks her teeth. 'I did enjoy it.'

I try to snatch my hand away, but she pulls it into her lap. Into her crotch. I can feel the warmth and dampness through the denim. I can't breathe now. I want to see what's under there. Can't even think about a young stiff cock now. Just a young, soft cunt.

'I liked being helpless like that, you see. It's like being a toy. He just did what he wanted, just undid my shirt at first, pulled down my knickers. That made him hard. That's when I realised it was fun.'

She's staring over my shoulder now, dreamily, rubbing my hand up and down her crack.

'Go on.' My voice is husky with lust now.

'He didn't touch my tits for ages, or, you know, my – here –' She presses my hand so hard that my knuckles grind against her, pushing between her pussy lips. 'until I was gagging for it – and then he showed me his huge, hard cock and he –'

'I still don't get it, Robin!' I hold my hand up to stop her. 'You've run away from there. You've come to me.' I need to regain some kind of upper hand here. 'So did he hurt you?'

'Oh, hurting me was the best bit! When he smacked me.' She jumps off the bed, dances across the room, juts her hips from side to side like a Cheeky Girl and smacks herself on the bottom, pat, pat, then harder on each thigh, making the flesh wobble. My mouth drops open. There are two red, hand shaped marks on her skin. 'You wouldn't believe how good it felt. That smarting, stinging feeling. Then the warmth, spreading through you. You can't wait for the next one –'

'I don't believe it.' I sniff and cross my legs primly. 'That kind of punishment is plain weird.'

So why is my pussy wet?

'Not weird! Wonderful! Christ, I've been *dying* to tell someone!'

She's vibrating with energy. No wonder that dirty old man salivated over her night after night. She's gorgeous. Those jutting breasts, those obscene shorts leading the eye straight to the cleft between her legs. She looks good enough to eat. I shift about, my pussy lips rubbing urgently together under my tight black skirt. Robin's nipples are taut against her vest. Mine are hard against my sweater.

Robin comes and strikes a pose in front of me as if she's about to give a lecture. But all I can look at are those nipples. 'He knew exactly what he was doing, you see. The funny thing is, that the tighter he ties you, the more powerless you are, and the better it feels. The ties leave pink bracelet marks round your wrists, so you're reminded all day when you're at work, and no-one will know. '

Robin giggles and bends to snap on the bedside light. Her back is to me and I can see the curve of one sex lip bursting through her shorts.

'Go on, tell me what he did to you,' I say, grabbing her and pulling her back to me. '*Show* me.'

She smiles again, one hand on her hip. 'OK. But you'll have to do it. Tie me up.'

I swallow hard. Her crotch is on a level with my eyes. 'What with?'

'How about your stockings?' She bends down, slides her hand up my leg under my skirt. 'I know you're wearing them, even in this heat.'

She's right. Still looking at her I cock my leg and slowly peel down my stocking. My face is burning, my stomach tight with excitement. Robin is watching me, her cat's tongue slicking over her lower lip. I hitch the tight skirt up towards my own crotch, and Robin's eyes gleam, but we don't speak.

When I've unrolled both stockings Robin lies down on the bed, spreads herself open, and waits.

'Tie me tight, like he did.' Still she's licking her lips. 'I want you to hurt me.'

'I don't know –'

'Please, Linda.' Robin pouts like a spoilt child. 'I want you to see what it's like. You can be my mistress.'

Her firm breasts jut upwards, the nipples already elongated and taut. So that's what the landlord saw, captive in his back bedroom. Sex on a plate, but not with a whore. Oh no. With a perfect angel. My little dolly, to play with whenever I like.

Barely thinking, I push her vest up first, to see those juicy breasts. See what the sleazy landlord saw. My pussy clenches, sending shivers right through me. That fresh, nubile body begging him to punish her. He must have thought he'd died and gone to heaven.

Suddenly I know what to do. I grab Robin's arms, wind the stocking round her wrists, and lash them to the rounded bedpost of the childish single bed.

Robin yanks at the restraints. 'Oh, they're very tight, Linda! I can't get away!' She starts to toss from side to side, her breasts wobbling delightfully, the nipples hard and red, the muscles in her arms straining. 'He didn't do it this tightly –'

Anxiety flashes through me, but then I see how Robin's tongue flickers with obvious pleasure as she struggles. As she flails about Robin kicks me hard, and a burst of energy surges through me. Quickly I unzip and yank down her little shorts, moaning with pleasure to see the soft crack, not waxed and bare as I'd imagined but with a neat line of pubic hair running over the crack. My own pussy contracts with savage desire. I tie the other stocking round one of her ankles and tie that to the bed. If I leave the other one free she can still offer me her bum.

'What are you going to do to me, Linda? Are you going to keep me here all night?'

Her bottom is rolling now, squashing against the blanket, lifting frantically to show the black seam between the cute butt cheeks.

'Would you like that? But oh dear, I'm not a man, Robin. I can't fuck you like your landlord did.'

I stare at her, spread-eagled on the bed, legs wide open, struggling, whining.

'You could find a way to fuck me. You know, use something. You could be him.' Robin gasps as she continues to thrash about, rubbing herself eagerly up and down the rough blanket. 'But I want it to turn you on, Linda. I think you're a goddess.'

My arm comes up and I slap Robin hard on the rump. The prime, tender flesh ripples under my hand. Robin squeals. 'So stop moving, young lady, while I decide what you deserve.'

'I'm not a young lady. I'm a filthy little tart! That's what he told me.'

I smack my hand down again, loving the sharp sound ringing out in the little bedroom, loving Robin's responding yelp. She jerks off the bed, then I smack her again. 'Keep totally still, filthy little tart, otherwise you're in trouble.'

Robin goes rigid, exaggeratedly obeying orders, and I stand over her, enjoying another surge of this strange new unaccustomed power. It bunches up inside, spiking through my cunt to make it throb with wanting.

'This is going to be so good, Linda,' Robin murmurs into the thick silence.

I shove one knee between her legs. Robin lifts her bottom off the bed, pushing her puffy little pussy at me. I stroke up her thighs towards it. Her skin is so warm. I push my fingers up towards the deep crease waiting there, tangle them in the soft bush. My own pussy is really wet.

With one hand buried inside her, I slap her other cheek again, feel the skin go hot. Christ, I'm out of breath. I unzip my skirt and fling it to one side. My knickers are soaking now. I whip them off too, and there's that horny smell again, my own this time, so intoxicating.

I lean forwards, pull Robin's thighs further apart, and now I can see the secret slit, the vivid red promise as the sex lips open, and without thinking I nudge the tip of my

131

nose in, forcing the lips further open, feeling the warm wetness on my face. A ripple of delicious shock goes through me to inhale another woman's scent. This must be what animals in the jungle do – but do the females go round sniffing each other's bottoms?

Robin's sex feels like silk against my nose. I've never kissed another woman before, let alone licked her cunt. I let my tongue slide over the slit, feeling Robin tense and shiver as I sweep once, twice, up over the furls of her sex, feeling the bump of the little clit. I rub my hand against my own pussy, scrape one finger against my own clit, everything contracting and squeezing urgently to come, now, straightaway. But it's too soon. I snatch my hand away, and start tasting her again, lapping like a cat cleaning her kitten, making the girl twitch and groan with every stroke.

'Am I your slave now, Linda?'

I jerk away, irritated at the interruption. 'Hush your mouth!'

'Please, Linda,' she whimpers, 'spank me again!'

'Don't tell me what to do, slave!' I force Robin's legs further open. 'For speaking you get punished. No more licking.'

'Oh, I'm sorry, Linda. But please! I'm creaming myself here!'

'You're here for my pleasure, remember!'

But I'm horribly close to coming. I must stop touching myself. I stare again at Robin's gaping slit, the puffy lips, the curls tight with moisture. I grab my flimsy lace knickers, roll them between my palms until they're a thin rope. Holding each end of the silky rope I slice it quickly up Robin's slit. She screams and arches, tipping herself upwards, offering herself desperately.

I scrape the knickers down hard, knowing that the unyielding fabric will be slicing right over the sensitive clit, scraping at the most tender parts. Robin's clit is turning bright red. I start rubbing this prop faster up Robin's cunt, thrilling to see her jumping and writhing about on the bed.

I yank the knickers away and, as Robin howls in frustration, bucking off the bed, I slap her hard again on her exposed buttock, then dangle the knickers, tickling them over her wriggling body, up towards the straining breasts, those big, accentuated nipples.

Robin won't stop wriggling. The only way to stop her is to sit on her. I settle myself astride my slave, but as my over-heated pussy meets Robin's, I nearly come there and then. I'm nearly mad with the feel of another woman's sex arousing me like this. Now I can't keep still. I crawl over Robin until I reach her moist, inviting mouth, and I press mine down. Her wet tongue flickers, probing inside my mouth, and now my climax is only seconds away.

'Your task, slave, before I even think of letting you go.' My voice is thick with desire as I grope for what I want. I crawl up her face until my pussy is over her mouth. 'Now lick me.'

I can feel Robin's warm breath on my pussy. And then the licking starts. Soft, almost feathery caresses over my pussy lips, which pulse quietly, Robin's wet tongue flicking up the crack then smoothing itself flat over the swollen lips.

My head is spinning. So much hornier with a girl. I spread my legs open further, seeking more intense pleasure.

'You taste so sweet, Linda.'

I moan and strain, pressing down as Robin's tongue laps faster, sensations sizzling in my cunt as Robin seems to suck my entire pussy while her tongue probes, forcing its way further in like a mini dick, then pulling back so that I grind harder into her face.

She touches my clit and it's like an electric prod. I can't help it. I jerk frantically. Now she's sucking again, so mercilessly. I rock faster, my legs open wider.

I can hear Robin's saliva as she feasts on my pussy. She's stopped circling and sucking and she's pushing her

133

tongue in hard like a cock, flicking it from side to side, sliding over the clit as it thrusts in and out. She's working me to a frenzy.

Here I come. I grip the bed post, draw my hips back in a final glorious convulsion and my cunt, my whole body draws in tight as I come, pushing into Robin's face, smearing my juices all over her, rubbing on and on until after the climax has faded.

'What about me?' she whimpers, shivering as I climb off her.

I want to hold her. But I don't want the game to stop. 'I'm going to put the supper on, Robin. And you, my pretty, are going to wait right here.'

Her luscious mouth pouts up again. 'Not fair!'

'Then maybe, if you're very good, we can do it all over again!' I pause in the doorway. 'Just one thing, young lady. References. If it was all so good at your last place, why did you have to leave?'

'Got chucked out!' She smiles, stretches her leg perfectly like a ballerina. 'The wife came back early from some business trip, didn't she? *Honey, I'm home!*' She chuckles. 'Found me tied up on their four-poster, legs wide open –'

'Pussy spilling all that rude redness!' I gasp. 'God, I can just see it! What else did she see?'

'Joe on top, of course. Fucking me.'

I can see it all, and it's making me horny, the woman in the pinstripes watching, the man's buttocks thrusting in between these lovely legs. My Robin's legs. I come back to her, tickle my knickers over her breasts, over the mound of her crotch.

'Never mind. It's just me and you now.'

Robin closes her eyes. 'Hurry back, Linda.'

'Oh, we've got all night.' I can't resist bending over and kissing my new lodger, tangling her tongue with mine. 'And you're going to be my new plaything.'

134

# Perfection
## by Cathryn Cooper

They'd become friends years ago in the days when their men-folk had been golfing partners. From then on they'd shared worries, triumphs and babysitters, socialised a lot with their partners and with each other. The three of them lunched together and shopped together, and once a month on a Thursday evening they dined together. Each woman took her turn to host the event in her own place, cooking and preparing everything themselves.

This evening, mellowed by good food, wine and the atmosphere of a room lit only by aromatic candles, they began to talk about what they were presently doing in their lives, their hopes for the future and how things had been in the days when they'd first met. It hurt to talk about their husbands in the days before they had departed, but naturally the subject of sex was eventually mentioned.

'I'm in the market for a younger man,' said Crystal, her dark eyes warm as brandy in the candlelit glow.

The others laughed. 'Hussy!'

'Well I suppose there's no point in having an affair with an older man,' said Josie, tossing her head so that her red hair suddenly seemed to burst into flame.

As the oldest, Greta was more circumspect. 'Hmm. I don't know about that. It depends if they can keep up the pace. I'm no hot totty teenager, but I've got experience! A toy-boy could learn a lot from me. An older man just wouldn't be able to keep up!'

They laughed at the joke, but their eyes glazed over with bittersweet memories, youthful distractions when they'd sighed for a look from a handsome boy and longed to be grown-up. Each slipped momentarily into another world, the one before they'd had husbands, families and responsibilities.

'No,' said Crystal shaking her head. 'None of us want an older man. Not now.'

'I had an affair with an older man when I was eighteen,' said Josie. As though only just realising what she said, she blushed and lowered her eyes. The others noticed and were instantly intrigued.

'Tell us,' said Crystal.

Greta leaned forward, her blue eyes bright with interest. 'Yes. Do tell.'

'Alright.'

Josie studied the table. For a moment it seemed to the others that she was unable to continue. The moment was short lived. She took a deep breath and collected herself before she began.

'He lectured in Greek history. I'd always loved the subject so was conceited enough to think I would have no trouble finishing the course and passing my exams. I found out to the contrary.

'It was one thing to read Greek classics and history as they related to the legends and the Trojan wars and such like. It was different to be asked to dissect and diagnose occurrences and modern counterparts on paper.

'Besides that, I was being invited to a lot of parties and was enjoying going to them.'

'Were you getting laid?' Crystal asked. There was a hint of sarcasm in her voice but envy in her eyes.

'Of course I did – once or twice. But they were one night stands and not terribly satisfactory – the fumblings of green fruit and all that.'

Greta smiled. 'And the tutor was definitely not green fruit. A little over-ripe perhaps?'

The others laughed. Josie smiled and a far away look came to her eyes.

'OK, his skin was as scored as an autumn apple. I used to think I would like to peel it away and find the smoother skin underneath it – the skin of his youth. I suppose thinking like that is all part of wanting to know someone better; knowing what's underneath and knowing about their past.

'His eyes were very blue and seemed to miss nothing. Like a lot of the students he taught, he wore his hair long and had a beard to match. It was bright blond – almost gold – but it had white streaks running through it. Not that it mattered. It flowed around him like a golden halo, and it was soft – very soft, very silky.

'Some of the other students – especially the fellas – made comments about him trying to hold onto his youth and why didn't he act and look his age. But of course they had their reasons for saying that. Whenever Cado was in the room he was the only man there as far as we girls were concerned.

'There was a husky harmony in his voice and an alluring brightness to his eyes. We were drawn to him and sat enthralled as he deliberated about the reasons why modern civilisation venerated the one that had flowered in Ancient Greece.

'He pointed out to us how many people and civilisations looked on Ancient Greece with envious eyes. Perfection, he said, was seen in its teachings, its scions, even in its buildings.'

137

'What about him,' asked Greta impatiently. 'Never mind what he or you lot believed in, what did you get up to with him?'

Josie licked away the dryness of her lips. 'I will tell you. Cado, you see, wanted perfection in humans as well as discerning it in an ancient civilisation. We didn't always give him that perfection. I was as imperfect as everyone else and ended up being called to his study after getting ticked off for not completing an assignment he had set us.

'He opened the door and bid me enter. The room was shabby, but I pretended to be genuinely interested by the décor. I gazed at the piles of papers, books and coffee cups. There was an ancient leather chesterfield in one corner. Most of the walls seemed to consist of nothing but bookshelves.

'Feeling his presence behind me was like being warmed by a coal fire. I felt the heat of his body on my back. I knew he was studying me, his eyes running over my body, perhaps assessing my shape and how my skin might feel; how I might respond if he touched me. Just being alone with him made me tremble with trepidation. Once the door was closed, he moved closer to me.

'"Josie, isn't it?"

'I replied that it was. He didn't say anything for a moment but hung his head slightly as though he were examining the hole in the carpet. I turned round. His hands were clasped tightly behind his back and I remember thinking, "what is he holding in them?"'

'What was he holding?' asked Greta.

Josie smiled. 'His courage.'

'"I expected better of you," he said. "I expected something close to perfection."

'"I'm sorry. I'm truly sorry!"

'I couldn't believe how emphatic I sounded. I hadn't wanted to disappoint him. "I want to be perfect," I said.

138

'Something about his eyes changed as he looked at me. "Do you really mean that?"

'"Yes."

'He nodded thoughtfully. "Then we will start again," he said. "I will instil in you the discipline you need. You will accept that discipline and in doing so, you will grow in stature and maturity. Do you agree to this?"

'I told him that I did. It was then that my education truly began. First I was to take off my clothes. I did it without hesitation. I so wanted to please him and be worthy of his idea of perfection.

'I stood trembling, lean and firm and tingling with excitement. He told me to look at my reflection in a full length mirror.

'The cool smoothness of his corduroy jacket briefly touched my back when he came to stand behind me. I sucked in my breath and saw my nipples grow. Transferring my weight from one hip to the other, I felt the sweet wetness erupt between my legs.

'"See?" He placed his hands on my shoulders. "It is through this flesh that I will ignite your mind."

'He took my hand and told me to bend over his desk. I did as he asked.

'"How does it feel?" he asked 'I told him that the leather of the desk top was cold to my nipples. I told him my breasts were flattened against the desktop and that its edge was nudging against my sex. Besides telling him that the carpet felt gritty beneath the soles of my naked feet, I also told him that my belly was sticking to the desk.

'"And which part of your body is most in touch with the world around you, Josie?" he asked

'"My mind?"

'"Ultimately," he replied. "But your mind gains perception through your naked bottom. Your buttocks are merely in touch with the air around them. Because of that it is sending more explicit messages to your brain than any

139

other part of your body. It is telling your brain that it is vulnerable. After all, it is only logical that the roundness of a woman's behind can attract a caress, a slap, or an act of buggery. So your mind is in tune with it...perfectly in tune."

'I closed my eyes, longing for him to touch me. He spoke for some time before his hand ran down my back. I remember trembling as he fondled my bottom.

'I knew the discipline would come, in fact I found myself yearning for it. He used a ruler and quoted something from Homer each time the ruler smacked my ass. I remember gasping.

'"Six to start with," he said.

'"More," I moaned. I couldn't help it you see. He'd awoken something in me, something I hadn't known was there.

'"More. Yes. More," he said. I waited for the blows. Instead I heard the sound of running water. "Raise yourself slightly," he said. I did so. He slipped a bowl of ice-cold water beneath each breast. I gasped again. My bottom was on fire. My nipples were hardening in response to the chilled water. "Now you are experiencing both heat and cold in two different spheres of your body. You will raise your arms above your head and lie as flat to the desk as possible. I will not resume this discipline until you do this."

'I did it gladly, longing for his attention and also for his approval. I WANTED him to think me perfect.

'At the closing of my eyes, my senses were ignited. I heard the sound of the ruler disturbing the air. I heard it smack my flesh and felt the warmth of its contact. My behind stung. My breasts stung, but differently and yet both the same. This wasn't sex; it wasn't sleaze; it was purely and simply erotic, a delicious awakening of the mind, the body and the senses.

'I muttered unintelligible sounds before asking him if I was now perfect, perfect enough to entice him into my body.

'I heard the rustle of clothes before he entered me. The most amazing thing was that he did not touch my breasts or any other part of my body as he fucked me. Only his penis, his pubic hair and the front of his thighs touched my body. I understood what he wanted me to do. With my arms thrown over my head and my eyes closed, I was to concentrate only on the areas of my body that touched his. And I did concentrate. Sex can never be the same with one man as another, and yet the differences are relatively slight. With Cado it was completely different. It's hard to describe those initial shivers of apprehension as arousal becomes more intense, more urgent. Behind the darkness of my eyelids, I truly experienced my climax taking over my body. Waves of pleasure crept over my skin. I'm sure I could also feel it creeping along just beneath the surface. On one level it seemed to be touching me lightly, no heavier than the caress of a bunch of peacock feathers. On another level it was causing my blood to boil and turn to steam in my veins.

'When my orgasm came I shuddered but did not cry out. I knew he didn't want that. I held the experience within me. It had no sound because it had no form. It was part of me and would remain part of me forever. Cado gave me that.'

Josie smiled softly to herself. 'I don't care if I was only eighteen and he was more than twice my age. He was one of the most enduring experiences of my life – perhaps the only one.'

Her friends clapped.

'What a dark horse you are, Josie Thompson!' exclaimed Greta.

Crystal shook her head. 'Funny. I thought somehow that you were above that kind of thing.'

Josie grinned as she reached for her walking stick. 'I've tried most of the vices, Crystal, and I have to tell you, sex is

141

the most enduring of my memories. I can still dream, and still remember how it was. Sex is what's kept me going.'

Her friends nodded in unison.

'Here's to young men,' said Greta. They raised their glasses in a toast and drained the last of their wine. Another evening was over, another chance to relive the passion of their youth.

# Paddles
## by Caesar Pink

For the evening's activities Heather was dressed in a skin-tight rubber mini-skirt, a pair of three-inch spiked heels, and a half T-Shirt with the word 'Goddess' written on the front in silver glitter. The plan was to visit an S&M club in Manhattan called Paddles. Although this was hardly my first journey into New York City's just-barely-underground BDSM scene, I still felt a bit dubious about the whole idea. The way one might feel about going to church after a night of drinking or to the mother-in-law's house for a tea party. Heather on the other hand, occasionally felt the need for a public spanking. Don't ask why. I don't know the answer.

When I first explored the BDSM scene one of the first things that surprised me was that there was very little sex mingled with S&M play. Most people outside the scene tend to think of it as a sexual kink, but inside the scene it seems to be separated from sexual activities. It is rare to see people even kissing or caressing each other at public play parties.

The people in the scene take it all very seriously. They are very involved with their toys. On multiple occasions I have watched people present a show and demonstrate the contents of their portable toy boxes, often describing, with obvious pride, every paddle, whip, cuff, or God-knows-what other objects of playful cruelty. What was even more comical is the sincere interest their compatriots seemed to have in these demonstrations. To invent a new way to use a common household item as a spanking device is a highly respected achievement.

Perhaps the only thing more important than the toys is the fashions of S&M, which are often surreal costumes of intricate design. S&M parties are a form of theatre. A costume ball with their own designers and clothing outlets. At their best you see beautiful people in elegant erotic costumes fit for a sci-fi fantasy thriller. At worst, you find pasty old men whose bloated bellies roll down over their leather jock-straps and ballerina slippers.

The theatrical aspects of S&M relate to more than just the fashions. The acts of S&M are themselves a form of performance. Rope tying is considered a high art and its devotees study Shibari and other complex knot-tying traditions from Japan and China.

There is almost a new-age flakiness to it at times. Especially the 'safe, sane and consensual' contingent. Although, given the dangers involved in such activities, I suppose such a motto is a good thing, but once you announce to all that it is safe, then it becomes…well…safe. Without a little danger it all seems a little goofy. When you take away the sex, and then take away the danger, all that you are left with is the theatre.

Being a culture based on dominance and submission, it also lends itself to some fairly neurotic behavior. I once had to deal with a burly biker man who spent the evening following Heather around asking her if she 'wanted to join his leather family.' There is little that is more irritating than the manoeuvres of small-time cult leaders as they vie for new followers.

When I enter one of these scenes, I usually want to take some time to lie back and check things out. But in the BDSM scene there is always someone invading your space. Old men wanting women to hold their leash while they

144

walk on all fours, or fat foot-fetish freaks who want to sit on the ground like overgrown children while they massage and kiss a woman's feet.

On the night in question, we arrived at Paddles and paid the $50 cover charge. Once inside we went from room to room checking the place out. The main room has a few booths and a bar with stools, as in an old-fashioned diner. No alcohol was served, just soft drinks and bottled water. There were assorted hallways and small rooms with a variety of furniture used for bondage. One large room held some complex contraptions that looked like medieval torture devices and antique medical furniture. There weren't many people around. A few people wandered from room to room. There was a human-sized birdcage in which a muscle-bound man stood in waiting.

I was trying to avoid socialising so we sat on a bench in a dark corner. We listened to a man and woman discuss the fine details of using ping-pong paddles for spanking. The conversation revealed an in-depth knowledge of different types of wood and their pro and cons for spanking. The man had a blue gym bag in which he kept his stash of toys. The woman was a muscular blonde dressed in black. After a bit he asked her if she would be so kind as to spank him a bit.

After he took off his shorts, she placed his hands in leather cuffs that were attached to chains that dangled from the ceiling, leaving him standing, but slightly bent over. She began by holding a whip with thin flat strands of leather above his back, allowing the strands to tickle his ass. Then to warm him up she slapped his cheeks with the palms of her bare hands.

By this time a small crowd had gathered to watch the proceedings. An attractive young couple who looked like they were new to the scene sat by the doorway, a scruffy but well-seasoned couple stood near the back of the room, and the unavoidable rabble of single men who haunt such dens of iniquity were positioned throughout.

145

Slowly she began spanking him with the whip. Each slow lash gained in intensity. He took the pain with little more than a few muffled grunts. Her movements had a luxurious grace to them, like a ballerina with an axe to grind.

The performance seemed to whet Heather's appetite. I could tell she wanted to take part in some action. I, on the other hand, was feeling introverted. People came up and tried to initiate conversation and I answered in short, cool replies. Eager to send them on their way. A middle aged guy asked if we were new to the scene, obviously looking for fresh meat to play tour guide to. After he gave up, I tried to shrink into the corner so we didn't have to endure another come-on.

As the spanking continued and the room filled, I lead Heather out by her hand. We wandered about, taking in the sights. An obese man came up and asked me if he could massage Heather's feet.

'Not right now,' I answered.

We watched a young couple who were alone in a dark hallway. They kiss gently before he bends her over his knee and spanks her with his hand. It is a much more sensual performance, and is actually somewhat erotic to watch.

As the night continues I feel like everywhere we walk some lecher is trying to pull us into his debauchery. Few of them are people I would want to interact with. S&M can be liberating both physically and spiritually, especially one's first experiences, but often the action one sees looks as meaningless as doing the dishes.

As we wandered from room to room, I was feeling pressure from all sides. I knew Heather was frustrated and wanted to play. On the other side, every freak in leather was trying to make our acquaintance.

There was a troupe of about five single guys that had been following us around, as Heather was likely the most attractive woman in the place. Finally, sick of the whole

146

scene, I took a deep breath and decided to give everyone what they wanted. First, I took Heather to the cage. The man inside was muscular and appeared to be a light-skinned Latino. I made her put her hand inside the cage and caress his chest. Heather seemed surprisingly nervous. The caged man stared straight ahead without speaking a word as Heather's small hand stroked his chest and belly.

This small action seemed to bring a wave of excitement to the gang of onlookers, and the sexual tension froze them into silent attention. I told her to remove her hand from the cage and put it back in through a lower rung so she could caress his half-hard cock. Heather seemed on the verge of shaking as she ran her hand across his abdomen and gently ran her fingers down the length of his penis. I stood watching, giving her ample time to give him the pleasure of her touch. Of her own volition, she removed her hand and placed it back in the cage so she could again caress his chest and shoulders as if to thank him.

From that moment on, the crowd would not leave Heather out of their sight. The men had taken up positions around the room, but all eyes were trained on her. I moved Heather to the center of the room and placed a blindfold over her eyes. Pulling a piece of clothes-line rope out of my pocket, I bound her hands behind her back. In that vulnerable position I gave her a slow wet kiss on the mouth. Then bound and blindfolded, and standing alone in the middle of the room with all eyes glued to her form, I lifted her half T-shirt allowing her small breasts to be seen by all.

I moved to the sidewall leaving her to stand alone in her darkness with the knowledge that a room full of faces she couldn't see were gazing at her body. No one spoke. No one moved. The room was taken by an awed reverence as if we were in the sanctity of a service of pagan goddess worship. With this tension in the air, I let the minutes stretch on.

Finally, moving to her, I bent down and ran my fingertips from her ankles to her thighs. Her spiked heels made her legs appear luxuriously long. She trembled slightly at the touch. I placed my lips to her breast and sucked. Slowly moving my hand down her belly, I pulled her rubber skirt up high above her hips. Naked underneath she stood bare, knowing the crowd was viewing her, judging her, lusting after her.

She stood dutifully. Like a soft Greek statue come to life. I returned to my perch against the wall and savored the spectacle. Her lovely body exposed and filled with apprehension. I looked around the room at the tense expressions on the faces of the onlookers. As the minutes passed the tension was sickening. Everyone was excited and frustrated by the possibilities of what might happen next.

When I thought she might collapse I went to Heather and, from behind, kissed her neck and shoulders. Guiding her by the shoulders, I moved her towards a twentyish-looking black man who was among the original five that dogged our trail and now had formed a half-circle in the centre of the room.

With Heather standing a few inches in front of him, I instructed him to suck her breasts. He bent down and put his mouth on her nipple and sucked. After a few minutes, I pulled her away and guided her to the next man who gently licked and sucked her breasts. I passed her from man to man until all five had taken their turn. Having had the blindfold on for some time, Heather had lost all conception of where she was and who was giving her such intimate touches.

I guided her back to her spot in the middle of the floor. Only now I removed the blindfold. With her breasts still exposed and her skirt pulled up above her hips, she stood face to face with the crowd of lechers, both men and woman, all of whom stared at her as if she were a spectacle for their entertainment. Like a naughty child forced to stand at the head of the class; like in the dreams of being naked in public that many people have, she stood fully exposed. As

148

she met their gaze head-on, her expression was a mixture of indignant embarrassment and haughty contempt. As if to say, 'What are you looking at? Something you can't have?'

After about ten minutes I untied her wrists and led her towards the back wall. The wall was made of cold cement and covered with chafed black paint. She faced the wall with her palms against it; I took a small flat lather paddle from my pocket and began to slowly spank her.

This part of the performance required some willpower on my part. While psychological games that provide someone with a new experience are one thing, giving someone physical pain goes so much against my instincts that I have to mentally assure myself that this is what is desired.

It is strange how many women seem to want to be spanked. It seems to be a fantasy of every woman I meet. It is a mystery to me. Perhaps it is the stress of city life? The responsibility and regiment required of office jobs and the struggle for survival that makes women want to submit completely to such treatment? Or perhaps it is the dictates of feminism, which have made so many men into well-meaning wimps, that make women long for a man who will take control of their whole being? Either way it seems to be a rampant desire among 20-something females.

Once at an Imperial Orgy art and poetry ball, a friend of Heather's was dressed as a dominatrix and was giving playful spankings to the party-goers. This friend asked Heather if she wanted to be spanked. As Heather took her place, expecting a couple playful swats from her friend, a strange man came out of the audience and took the whip and began to lash her brutally. A group of about 50 people watched in shock. After a few minutes I left the room, not having the stomach for the brutality. After the spanking, Heather found me lying on some pillows on the floor watching experimental videos in another room. Her behind was covered in welts.

149

In a strange piece of synchronicity, on the same night a close friend in Utah was given an even more brutal caning at a party there. I was a bit taken aback by it all. Who are these women in my life?

Back at Paddles, I steadied my hand and delivered solid swats to Heather's behind. The sound of leather on skin echoed against the dungeon walls, and seemed to make Heather more excited. As the blows got harder, gasps of pain began to slip out of her mouth. Finally, exhausted, she fell to her knees. As I helped her up I whispered, 'Are you OK?'

She nodded her head, but she was soft as putty, and unstable as a newborn calf.

For one final act of humiliation, I led her to the main room and strapped her to a massive wooden contraption. She sat in an upright position with her arms spread out in a crucifix position. He legs were strapped in and spread wide open, leaving no secrets to the crowd of onlookers that had followed us to the new location.

I left the room, leaving her alone with the mob. Not a single person came near or dared to touch her. When I finally returned and freed her from her bondage, I instructed her to go and thank the five men who had sucked on her breasts.

Helping her to pull herself together, we walked out into the cold winter air. Heather seemed spent, but serene. As I drove she looked out the window. She seemed to feel a bit insulted, but was well aware that she got exactly what she wanted.

# Snookered
## by Stephen Albrow

The playful chink of the snooker balls came to a sudden halt, the second that Carla stepped through the door. The snooker hall was strictly a male preserve, but it wasn't just the sight of a woman that had surprised the members, so much as the outfit she was wearing that night. Her pleated black skirt was barely long enough to cover her patterned stocking tops, while her schoolgirl-style blouse was artfully unbuttoned, exposing a cleavage-crack of eye-catching depth. She felt a hundred eyes upon her, as she broke the silence with her slow, purposeful footsteps, her six-inch heels chiming loudly against the chalk-dust-spattered wooden floor.

'Fancy a game, love?' Her arrival had caused some real excitement.

'Yeah, fancy a game, love!' It was as if they'd never seen a woman before.

Carla smiled at her potential suitors, but strode deeper into the smoke-filled room, her perfume intoxicating every one of them. She was literally a breath of fresh air. The seductive scent of her Versace Crystal Noir had brought some much-needed femininity to the overwhelmingly masculine room, overpowering the unpleasant stench of stale beer, fags and week-old sweat.

There were twenty tables crammed into the hall, every one of them occupied. The players followed her progress, as she wandered through the maze of tables, her full hips swaying from side to side. Was she someone's wife or girlfriend? Had the manager hired a stripper? What else could explain why a woman like her would have encroached upon their exclusively male environment?

She certainly had a sense of purpose about her, judging by how immaculate she looked. Her long, blonde hair had a straight-from-the-salon gleam about it, while her make-up brought out the best in her pretty features, highlighting her big blue eyes and made-for-giving-blowjobs lips.

Games resumed all across the snooker hall, players leaning over tables to pot reds and blacks. But still they kept one eye upon her, eager to know what her purpose was. She came to a halt by table fifteen, where two young men were in the middle of a frame. They looked at her with puppy-dog eyes, uncertain whether to make eye contact with her, or whether to do what everyone else was doing and stare, instead, at the mystery woman's endless legs or the never-ending crack between her bra-less breasts.

'All the tables are full, so can I play with you guys?' asked Carla, speaking in a voice like honey. They looked at each other, then nodded yes, but neither really knew what he was agreeing to. Was she asking to play a game of snooker with them, or was there something even more exciting on offer?

'Let's see how good you are,' said one of the guys, handing her his snooker cue.

Carla picked the chalk off the side of the table, then rubbed it all over the tip of the cue, but even that had a sexual feel about it – one hand on the shaft, as she toyed with the tip. Her tongue was poking out of her mouth, sliding slowly round the circumference of her lips. The two young men could tell she was a tease, for sure. When she

152

blew off the excess chalk dust, it was like she was blowing them both a deep-throat kiss.

'Oh, I'm pretty good,' said Carla, then she leant across the table, lining up a red into the centre pocket. The guys stood behind her, watching her skirt ride up above her stocking tops, as she bent right over and made the pot. Her positioning was perfect, leaving her an easy black into the left corner pocket, but one that would force her to lean even further across the table.

She moved into position, stretching far across the smooth green baize, with her curvaceous arse poking into the air. It was just how she had planned it to be, with her skirt rising higher as she stretched right out, exposing the creamy white flesh above her black nylon stocking tops and then the back of her tight black knickers.

The first wolf-whistle was quickly followed by a second, then a hundred whistles seemed to sound at once. 'Hey, love, you're putting me off my stroke,' complained a dark-haired man on the next-door table, as he craned his neck for a better view of Carla's lace-trimmed knickers. Carla revelled in the attention, giving her buttocks a gentle wiggle, as she thwacked the black into the corner pocket. The pot was greeted with a hearty cheer, as was Carla's next choice of shot. This time she faced the pack of wolves, as she bent down over the snooker table, giving them a full-frontal view of her voluptuous breasts, which were threatening to spill out of her too-tight blouse.

There were twenty games taking place just then, but Carla's seemed to be the only one that mattered. She took her time lining up the next red, even pausing to wink at her playing partners, before driving it into the far corner pocket. The cheer was even louder this time, because everyone was desperate for the break to continue, so they could watch her bending over the table again and again. But things were getting too raucous. As she bent down and flashed them her knickers again, the excited yells and wolf-whistles carried all the way to the manager's office.

It took him just a matter of seconds to size up the situation. 'We have a dress code here, madam,' he said, pushing his way through the crowd that had gathered round the table where Carla was playing.

Carla recognised her husband's voice straightaway, and she could sense the angry tone of it, too. He had always been a very jealous man, so her provocative outfit would not have pleased him. Two snooker players began to argue with him, telling him he should let her carry on playing, then everyone booed when he insisted the club was for members only and that this mystery woman was *not* a member. Butterflies fluttered in Carla's stomach, as she watched her husband's anger growing. She had been a bad girl, distracting him at his workplace, so a terrible punishment was sure to follow.

'Come this way, please, madam,' the manager muttered, wanting her out of there before anyone twigged she was his wife. Carla wanted to stay, but she dare not argue – she could see the steely look in his eyes.

Reluctantly, she gave her cue back to its owner, then she gave her audience a sheepish smile, as she followed her husband into the tournament room. Outside, in the main hall, it was just as if someone had switched out all the lights, the raucous excitement vanishing to nothing, as the beautiful woman was taken from them. But, inside the tournament room, things were just warming up, a palpable tension hanging in the air.

The room was newly refurbished, with just one snooker table in the centre and a wall of gleaming trophies at the farthest end. The balls were all racked up, all ready to play, so she took a cue from the stand and stepped tentatively towards the table, before bending down to line up a shot. Her husband had gone silent, which had the effect of unnerving her far more than if he had been screaming and

154

shouting. How angry was he about her showing off her body to his customers? He had always been a very conservative man, with a very rigid sense of what was right and what was wrong.

Still silent, he stepped up behind her. Her skirt had climbed above her knickers once again. She could hear the measured, heavy sound of his breathing, a chilling reminder of his ominous presence. She could feel the weight of his stare, as well. His eyes were boring a hole through the back of her knickers.

'Put down the cue, you slut,' he commanded, eventually breaking the stony silence.

Carla did as she was told to do, then rested her hands on the smooth green baize. Her eyes were fixed upon the trophy cabinet. She was too scared to look back at her husband. She heard the rustle of his nylon shirt, as he raised his arm to shoulder-height, then felt the bitter sting, as the palm of his hand struck the naked flesh between her stocking tops and knickers.

'That's for dressing like a whore,' the manager shouted, immediately spanking her thighs again. 'And that's for distracting my customers,' he yelled, before delivering another, firmer blow, this time to her shapely buttocks.

Carla closed her eyes, as her arse cheeks experienced a thrilling burst of pain, which was barely cushioned by her skimpy knickers. Her lips fell open and a groan burst out. Already her cheeks felt red and sore, and yet the punishment had only just begun.

'And that's for bothering me at work,' barked her husband, as his hand thrashed through the air once again. He struck the lower curve of her buttocks, hard enough to leave a bright red mark, before yanking her knickers down to the floor, baring her buttocks for further chastisement.

'You're a slut,' he shouted, executing another fearsome slap, which sent painful quivers through her exposed flesh. The sting was spreading all over now, going way beyond

155

the point of impact. Her arse cheeks might have been receiving each blow, but the shooting pains seemed to know no limits, reaching high up her back and far down her thighs.

'Yes, you're right, I am a slut,' she confessed, relishing the buzz she'd got from teasing the guys in the snooker hall. In her mind they were all lined up to fuck her. It was wrong for a married woman to be having such thoughts. But she couldn't fight her urges, her inner desires, however wrong they might be. She deserved to be punished. She *wanted* to be punished.

She raised her rear-end a little higher, imploring him to strike her again.

'One… Two… Three… Four…'

Joe started counting out the spanks, but he hadn't warned her how many were to come. She groaned and whimpered, a part of her desperate for the pain to end, but a bigger part of her wanting to be spanked so hard that she wouldn't be able to sit down for weeks.

'Nine… Ten… Eleven… Twelve…'

The spanks just kept on coming and her mind kept responding. The men were still there, lining up, wanting to put their dicks into her. She could see them in her mind's eye, feel them with every slap of Joe's hand. Her pussy dripped with juice, as she pictured herself taking prick after prick after prick inside her cunt.

'You're such a slut,' yelled Joe as he counted out another five blows.

Carla stood up and turned round. 'So, why don't you fuck me like a slut?' Her smile was the come-on, as lewd as her behaviour, daring him to do more, challenging him to at least try.

She spotted what she'd hoped to see – a massive bulge in her husband's jeans. She tugged down his zipper and unleashed his dick.

'Up on the table, bitch,' he demanded, giving her rump another slap. With a sweep of her arm, Carla pushed the snooker balls aside, mounted the table and spread her legs. His weight bore down upon her as he pushed himself in. She was wet, she was ready, her pussy muscles throbbing, drawing him in.

Carla stared up at the ceiling, a feeling of warmth flowing through her, along with a blissful sense of relief. The spanking and forceful penetration satisfied her deep inner need for hard, fast sex.

Every one of the men in the snooker hall would have been happy to have given her what she craved in the line of rough sex, but it wasn't them she wanted. It was Joe; it had always been Joe. It was just a case of rousing him from the gentle, good creature he usually was. Invading his working space always did it.

Gasps of pleasure poured from her lips, greeting each of her husband's high-speed thrusts. Her muscles convulsed around his swollen manhood, as it powered in and out of her hole, sparking pleasurable tingles throughout her deep, wet passage. She couldn't decide which she liked the most – the pleasurable feelings in her pussy or the excruciating twinges she felt as her aching buttocks chafed against the snooker table's surface. These powerful throbs were constant reminders of the spanking she had taken, her punishment for being such a bad girl. Her craving for dick had been so strong that night, she knew she would've been prepared to cheat on her husband, so, even now that he was fucking her senseless, and there was no longer any danger of her straying elsewhere, she still felt a need to be reprimanded. She still deserved to be made to squirm.

'Am I a bad girl?' she asked, as her husband pulled back, his lengthy cock sliding out of her cunt.

'You know you are,' he answered, his hips already moving forward again, ramming his fulllength back into Carla's gash. She sensed the tremors in his cockhead, as it

157

dug into the heart of her, then her insides were completely overwhelmed by the violent force of his ejaculation. Jets of hot moisture spurted from his helmet with a degree of venom that made it feel, to Carla, like a further bout of spanking. There was anger and aggression in this vast outpouring of sticky spunk. There was menace and fury in these orgasmic pulsations, which resounded deep within Carla's pussy, triggering her own climactic explosion.

A sequence of convulsions tightened Carla's pussy, then a warm wave of juices flowed from deep within her. She felt the moisture wet her inner thighs, as her whole body spasmed, writhing and twisting on the tabletop. Her breath grew faster, then she heard herself yelling her husband's name, as he entered her deeply once again. His full length powered through her churning orifice, the unforgiving force of this sudden thrust sending her climax right off the scale.

Carla begged her husband for mercy, unable to cope with the feelings any more. Too many sensations – some sensuous, some sore. The delicious explosion between her legs! The bitter sting in her arse cheeks! The rapid drumming of her overworked heartbeat! The multiple climax thundering through her body!

'I can't take it,' she yelled, drumming her fists against the tabletop, then her passion reached its zenith and rendered her dumb. A dizzying light appeared before her eyes, blinding her to everything but the fierce sensations, each contraction like a lightning strike. And there, at the centre of it all was the rigid length of her husband's prick, still pumping in and out of her, taking her to these blissful heights.

The dizzying light before her eyes began to fade. She smiled up into her husband's face. His muscular presence bore down upon her, crushing her against the bright green baize.

'So, have you learned your lesson?' he asked, a smirk appearing on his lips. His anger had faded as his balls drained dry.

'Yes, I've learned my lesson,' Carla promised, but even as she said it, she knew it was a lie. It wouldn't be very long before she misbehaved again.

Something very special had taken place that night, as she'd bent across the snooker table and been spanked into submission. It was something that she couldn't allow to happen only once, even if it did mean going against her husband's orders. It had been fun for her to be the bad girl, and there was no doubt that he'd enjoyed telling her off, otherwise he wouldn't have mixed in so much pleasure with the pain. So, for all his insistence that she learn her lesson, and for all her claims that she'd seen the error of her ways, Carla knew they were both already anticipating the bad girl's next act of naughtiness – and the fearsome, buttock-clenching, 'knickers down, bend over, miss' punishment that would follow!

# Rescue Me
## by Jean-Philippe Aubourg

Jill sighed as she saw there was another new email from Gareth. At first it had been amusing that they shared this little secret. It would never have come out, but for that one drunken Friday night fling last year. The sex had been forgettable, but what happened the following morning had not been.

Gareth had made a clumsy attempt to spank her, rolling her onto her front as they lay naked in his bed, slapping her bottom three times before she had the chance to leap up and away from his clutches. He was apologetic but not regretful, explaining how it was his kink, how a lot of his conquests loved it, and how he found the best way of broaching the subject was with actions, not words.

She gave him a few words to the effect that she would never humiliate herself by allowing a man to spank her, and if he had any respect for women he'd think very carefully before he ever slapped a bottom again.

Evidently he failed to take her philosophy to heart. Indeed, he seemed to take a perverse pleasure in telling her all the gory details of his subsequent lovers, their evident love of a good hard bottom-smacking, and how excited it got them. Jill was certain most, if not all, were made up, and she told him so. It didn't stop the emails though.

Jill took a deep breath and clicked the latest one open. It was a single paragraph.

'Saw that redhead again last night. Third time this month. In fact, we've talked about her becoming my permanent submissive. Great arse! Goes really red when she's been over my lap for a session!'

Jill clicked on reply: 'Red Lion, 7 p.m.. Just us.'

Four hours later they faced each other over the table of one of the pub's discreet booths. 'So what's up?' asked Gareth.

'Nothing special. I just thought you needed to get out more. You've been spending too much time with your imagination lately.'

'Far from it! No time for that, not with my new playmate!'

'Oh, you mean your 'redhead?'' Jill used her fingers to put quotation marks around the last word. 'Yes, you two have been busy. And she's perfect for you! So perfect, you could almost have created her yourself!'

'Do I detect a note of disbelief, my pet?'

'Really? Now why would I doubt that you've found a woman who actually enjoys having a male chauvinist pig inflict pain on her for his selfish sexual gratification? Of course such women exist! And of course, they're easy to find!'

'I admit, it used to be hard, in spite of my obvious attractions.'

Jill snorted. Though in his mid-forties, with a firm body and a sparkle in his eye, Gareth wasn't unappealing. 'But the internet is a wonderful invention. There are all sorts of websites and chat rooms where like-minded people can make contact.'

'You mean pervert guys like you can swap wank fantasies!'

'Do not scoff! I've found three women that way, all of them very good playmates. The last two were from an

162

excellent site, spanking mates-dot-com. Latest one's a City banker, spends all day dealing with massive amounts of money, so finds handing over control to me the perfect way to unwind. You should try it!'

'That'll be the day!'

'No, really, you should try it!'

'Look Gareth, that night was all very nice, but as I explained, I'm not looking for anything long-term right now, and I'm definitely not into…'

'Hold on, that's not what I meant. If you're so certain that no woman could really be genuinely into this…'

'…or could be cured, if she thinks she is!'

'…or could be cured! OK, if you're so sure, then find me one and rescue her!'

'What?'

'You heard me. Make contact online with a submissive woman, convince her of the massive mistake she's making, then present me with the evidence that you've converted her back to what you think is normality, and I'll admit you were right.'

'Is that all?'

'Okay. And buy you dinner at the restaurant of your choice, regardless of price or exclusivity.'

'Sounds like a deal.' Mentally, Jill was already making a reservation at the Ivy.

'Of course, if you don't,' Gareth went on, 'you need to pay a forfeit.'

'Forfeit?'

'Yep. Say, if you haven't rescued one of these poor submissives within a week, then I get another chance to redden your bum.'

'What?'

'Skirt up, knickers down, over my lap for a proper spanking.'

Jill thought carefully. The prospect of being indecently assaulted did not appeal one little bit, but could she back

163

down now, and demonstrate a total lack of faith in her sisters' commitment to the feminist cause? 'Okay,' she said, after a short pause, 'deal!' They shook hands and looked at one another smugly.

The next morning was Saturday. Jill woke up trying to brush away the fog of a red wine hangover, and groaned as she remembered the bet. Sitting up in bed, Jill took in the horrible prospect of what would happen to her if she lost. Getting up and into her dressing gown, she shuffled to the living room and opened her laptop.

Jill found the website and looked at its front page. At the top was a picture of a buxom blonde, naked apart from a black bra, balanced over the lap of a balding man, his hand raised, about to deliver a spank, the girl's face a picture of posed horror. Beneath the photo was a list of rooms available inside, and instructions on how to register and log on.

She followed the instructions, eventually registering as Jill36. As she went through the process it occurred to her that there were no checks to determine she really was who she claimed to be. 'Gareth could be talking to anyone' she murmured with a chuckle.

Once inside, she chose to go straight to the main room. The list told her it had a hundred and twenty-three people inside. She scanned it up and down, but was immediately hit by three personal messages, all from men. She politely declined, saying she wasn't interested. Two took the hint, but one wouldn't stop asking personal questions about who spanked her, and how, until Jill eventually found an ignore button and got rid of him.

She sent a few personal messages of her own to people with female profiles, but found most either ignored her or fired back with the same kind of questions, asking for more lurid details. 'You're fooling no-one!' she laughed, as she hit ignore for each one.

She checked out the lesbian room, and started a couple of decent conversations. But, while she was convinced these were real women, one was dominant while the other was in California, neither suitable for her purpose. She politely said her goodbyes and joined the room for UK chatters.

She was meeting with the same fruitless response, until another personal message box popped open. 'Hi!' was all it said.

It came from 'fiona31', the lower case indicating this person considered herself a submissive, as Jill now understood. She had naturally written her own name with a capital, so everyone assumed she was a dominant mistress, which suited her fine.

'Submissive, 31, UK' said fiona31.

'Where in UK?' asked Jill.

'London.'

So far, so good. 'So what are you into?'

'Spanking and humiliation.'

Perfect. Time to start the charm offensive.

'So what do you like about it?'

'It gets me hot! I love going naked over a lap, waiting for it to start! Love corner time too!'

'Corner time?' Jill was unfamiliar with the phrase.

'Corner time. Stood in the corner, hands on head, waiting for my Master to decide when my punishment will start.'

'And what does he use on you, when he decides it's time to start?'

'He puts me over his lap, naked, and smacks my bottom. Then he bends me over the back of a chair and uses a heavy strap. Then I have to touch my toes in the centre of the room, for a hard caning, at least eighteen strokes, usually more.'

'Wow!'

'Then I pay him tribute.'

'Tribute?'

'Tribute. With my mouth, then my pussy. I kneel and suck him till he's as hard as possible, then I get on all fours and he takes me from behind.'

Yes fiona31, I'm sure he does, thought Jill. But what she typed was: 'Wow! Does that really turn you on?'

'Just before he comes, I come too, like an express train! Sorry Babe, I've got to go! See you again soon!'

'Wait!' typed Jill, but as soon as she pressed return, a message that fiona31 had logged off was flashed up.

'Damn!' Jill cursed, 'she has potential! I just need a few more minutes to sow the seeds of doubt.' Looking at her watch, she realised she had been surfing for three and a half hours. 'Time flies, when you're saving sisters' souls!' she muttered, and went to run a bath.

As she lay in the water, bubbles resting on her large brown nipples and heavy breasts, Jill wondered what fiona31 was like. First she imagined her as a blonde, with blue eyes and a model figure, but quickly decided that made her as much of a fantasist as the men who had bombarded her with messages. No, she would be dark, or light brunette, with a face that was more interesting than classically beautiful. Her figure would be curvy and voluptuous, the kind so many men seemed to like, in spite of everything the fashion magazines preached, with a bottom that wobbled when her Master spanked it, and hips he could grab as he took her ruthlessly from behind.

Jill imagined that bottom turning red as fiona31's Master balanced her across his lap, then put her back in the corner while he fetched his strap. And after the strap, the cane, then total sexual submission, fiona31 kneeling to suck cock, then offering herself in the most submissive position possible, so her Master could take her, hard and fast, before discarding her like an empty plate after a gourmet meal...

Jill's whole body tensed, and she shook with a feeling, which although familiar, she hadn't experienced for some time. As she came down from her orgasm, water splashing onto the tiled floor, Jill realised her right hand had travelled down to her sex without her even being aware of it.

Confused by her reaction to fiona31's story, Jill got out of the bath and towelled herself down. OK, it was a powerful image, but it was still all wrong for a woman to let a man do that to her. fiona31 had to be saved from herself.

Jill dropped into the chat room again that afternoon, but there was no sign of fiona31. Nor again on Sunday morning, afternoon or evening. So eager was Jill to speak to her, she even considered logging on at work on Monday, but fought the urge and rushed home with a purpose at the end of the day.

She logged on without even bothering to start dinner, and scanned the list of names. Yes! There she was! 'Hi!' typed Jill.

There was a gap of some seconds before fiona31 replied with an equally jaunty 'Hi!'

'Good weekend?' asked Jill, not sure how else to start the conversation.

'Great! Master gave me a real thrashing on Saturday night!'

Jill felt her stomach lurch as she read the words. That had to be horror and revulsion. It certainly wasn't excitement! 'What happened?'

'As I described to you, that's exactly what he did. But while he was caning and strapping me, I told him all about you.'

'Really?' Jill was genuinely taken aback. There was another pause before the next answer came.

'Really. I've stripped now. I'm naked.'

'Why?'

'Because that's what I was ordered to do the next time we chatted. And what my Master says goes.'

Jill was intrigued, but this time she really believed the girl had stripped naked, and had a strange feeling of elation

167

at the thought of the power someone else had over her. 'What do you look like?'

'Long curly hair, 34b breasts, slim, long legs. Got a lot of freckles!' Jill's previous images of fiona31 were replaced by a new one.

The pair chatted on into the evening, Jill listening, asking questions, and trying to learn everything she could about fiona31. She discovered that she lived in almost the same part of London as her, just a short bus ride away, and that she had a job with some degree of responsibility, although fiona31 was cagey about saying exactly what it was. She had been introduced to spanking by a boyfriend at the age of twenty-six, a boyfriend who had apparently taken her for granted and eventually left her, albeit with a desire for further physical chastisement. She had dabbled with bisexuality, sleeping with a girl while at university and indulging another boyfriend's desire for a threesome with another woman, neither experience she deemed unpleasant.

Before she realised it, Jill's watch had ticked round to ten-thirty, and she began to feel tired. Securing a promise from fiona31 to be back on line the following night, the women said their goodbyes and logged off. Over a quickly thrown-together meal, Jill made notes about her new friend and her next steps.

Their chats continued every night for rest of the week, fiona31 revealing ever more intimate details of herself – how her Master enjoyed anal sex from time to time, how he had once made her stand to have her breasts whipped with a multi-tailed whip, how he enjoyed watching her bring herself to orgasm with a vibrator – all the while claiming to be naked while she surfed.

By Friday, Jill was ready to move in. The submissive had just described a severe session with a wooden paddle, when Jill dropped her killer question: 'fiona31, have you ever thought why you enjoy all this?'

'No? No idea, just know it gets me hot!'

'Just a thought – maybe you're doing it to indulge your man's passion, because you're desperate for his approval, and terrified he'll leave, and you'll be alone.'

'Eh?!?'

Jill had expected fiona31 to log off and never be seen again, at least not by her. Instead she stayed, talking over what Jill had said. The conversation went on until the early hours of the morning. Finally, fiona31 agreed to sleep on it, and leave a message for Jill the next day.

Saturday morning, a week after she had started her search, Jill opened her laptop and checked her emails. Sure enough, there was a new mail from fiona31. Jill's fingers trembled as she opened it.

'Babe! You're so right! I had no idea I was trapped in this constant cycle of one-way relationships! I'm going to tell Master that he isn't my Master any more, and he can find himself a new fool to be his submissive!

'I won't be logging onto the site again, but I owe you so much, and I want to say thanks. Would you like to come round for a meal and a bottle of wine tonight? Email me yes, and I'll give you the address.'

Yes! I've got him! Just within a week! I'll have dinner with fiona31 – or rather, Fiona – and persuade her to meet Gareth. Then he can buy us BOTH dinner at the Ivy, to make up for his persistent mistreatment of women.

Jill fired back the email and quickly received one in reply. A few hours later, she was outside a smart Victorian block in a nearby suburb, clutching a pricey bottle of red wine. She found Fiona's name under her doorbell and rang it.

'Jill? Come in!' chirped a friendly female voice over the intercom, as the door was buzzed open.

Jill climbed three flights of stairs to the flat. She was a little surprised to find the door already open, but assumed it was for her convenience. She closed it behind her and followed the sound of subtle jazz from the living room – and stopped dead in her tracks.

Fiona, or at least the woman she assumed was Fiona, was right there – standing naked in the corner.

Her figure was as trim as she had described it, her breasts small and high, the cherry red nipples hard. A neatly trimmed thatch of pubic hair led to slim thighs and long legs. Her freckled face was cast downwards and her hands were meshed somewhere inside her thick mop of long red curls, which tumbled loosely over her shoulders. But, shocking as that sight was, it was the figure seated in an armchair next to her that drew the gasp of shock from Jill.

'Gareth! What the hell are you doing here?'

'You should read my emails more carefully Jill, instead of dismissing them as works of fiction. You might have recognised the hot little redhead I described, and with whom you've been chatting all week. And a very nice chat it was too, by all accounts!'

'But…but…she told me she was…'

'Giving me the elbow? After you'd opened her eyes to the error of her ways and convinced her it was only to indulge my lusts, not hers? If that's the case, why is she naked and waiting for me to begin punishing her? And why can't she wait for me to do this!'

With one deft movement, Gareth took Fiona by her waist and slipped her over his lap. His right arm came up and he began a brisk spanking of her tight cheeks. She gasped and quivered, but made no attempt to escape his clutches or the punishment.

'Hooking you up was a bit of luck, but fairly straight forward' Gareth explained, without missing a beat. 'I knew you'd start on the website, and I knew it would take you time to find someone to take you seriously. I was also pretty sure you'd use your real name, so I told Fiona to watch out for a new arrival called Jill, who'd ask lots of questions, and eventually try to persuade her she didn't really like

170

spanking. She knew it was you after the first night. To be honest, I'm surprised you waited a week. OK, your turn!' As he spoke, he flipped Fiona back onto her feet, and directed her towards the corner, where she resumed her former position, but this time facing the wall, hands on head, red bottom glowing.

'M-my turn?'

'Come on Jill, a deal's a deal! Your week's up, and you've clearly failed to convert Fiona to your idea of normality. Get your skirt up and get over my lap!'

'But you set me up! Both of you!'

'I admit we were a bit devious, but you believed what you wanted to hear. And face it, you were never going to succeed anyway.'

Jill had no idea why she didn't walk out. Instead she found herself walking towards Gareth, shedding her coat and the wine bottle as she went. Almost in a dream, she felt her dress being lifted at the back as she slid over Gareth's lap and settled into place, her hands sinking into the carpet. Her knickers were slid down and her bottom totally exposed.

She held her breath as she waited for the first slap, admitting defeat to herself and to Gareth, and in a strange way, to fiona31.

The spanking was hard but mercifully short. Nevertheless, she wriggled and moaned throughout and afterwards.

Eventually she began to recover and was about to get to her feet, when she sensed a movement between her legs. My God, it was fiona31! Jill felt her sore cheeks being parted, and the other girl's hot breath as her face was lowered towards her sex.

Three minutes later she lay panting over Gareth's lap once more, an intense orgasm subsiding. 'Okay! You two may have a point. This bears further investigation.'

Sliding onto her knees, her skirt still bunched around her hips and her panties stretched tight between her thighs, Jill's shaking fingers pulled Gareth's trousers open. He was rock hard as she slipped his manhood into the open. Rubbing it tenderly with her fingertips, she kissed the tip, then ran her tongue up and down its length, before slipping her lips over the head, and beginning to move her head up and down.

As she sucked, she heard fiona31 behind her. 'Dinner's on me tonight, as promised. The Ivy OK? Hang the expense, I got a massive bonus from the bank last month, and they know me well enough to take a last-minute booking. And, after all,' she added, 'it's my second-favourite way for a lady financier to relax!'

# Show Me The Love
## by Landon Dixon

Jerry had been going out with Marion for a month when he decided to get really acquainted with her ass. He'd been first attracted to the petite, brown-haired, brown-eyed beauty by her big, round, fleshy backside, and now he wanted, needed to fully explore it – flail and fuck it, if possible.

He was concerned, though, about how she'd react when confronted/rear-ended with the full extent of his overwhelming butt fetish. He'd been careful with her so far – sex in all the conventional positions and orifices – because he was already thinking that maybe she was the 'one'; witty, warm, intelligent, loved football, with a good, firm set of tits and a wicked bubble butt – what more could one man ask for? Jerry could almost see himself settling down on a permanent basis with the girl.

But first he had to indulge his anal cravings, gauge her reaction. Like lemmings over a cliff, he just had to.

She was standing in front of the mirror on his dresser, her sun-burnished, rounded backside resplendently split up the middle by a sexy black thong. She was wearing nothing else but the erotic underwear and a smile, getting ready for her part-time job as a server at Laissez Faire, a sleazy night club on the East side. Her skimpy French maid outfit was lying at the foot of the brass bed Jerry was stretched out on.

He was naked, his cock hardening along with his resolve as he studied Marion's bold, bronze butt mounds.

'I don't like you working at that joint,' he said, watching her cheeks flex as she applied lipstick.

Marion puckered her lips and blew a kiss at Jerry's blond reflection in the mirror. 'Worried I'll meet some rich playboy?' she teased.

Jerry gripped his erection and stroked, fingers swirling over the veined length of his pulsing hard-on, eating up the girl's ripe, peachy bum with his hungry eyes. Her overstuffed seat cushions shone smooth and hot under the muted lights, gleaming orbs of taut, yet pliable flesh. 'I don't like you parading around in that outfit, wiggling your ass in front of all those drunks.'

'Can't be helped, darling. It pays the tuition. Just one more year and I'll have my diploma, be making scads of money. Until then...' She shrugged her shoulders, her cheeks jiggling enticingly.

Jerry slid off the bed and walked over to her, cock bobbing, pointing the way to her butt. He put his big hands on her shoulders, his big cock pressing against the heart-stopping swell of her buttocks. She patted his hand, then plucked a bottle of mascara out of her make-up bag and started applying it to her lashes.

Jerry's hands fell off her shoulders, and he took a step back. He stared down at her brazen booty, anger and lust combusting within him. He drew back a hand, hesitated, then whacked her ass, hard.

'Hey!' she yelped, grabbing the edge of the dresser, mascara tumbling onto the carpet.

He smacked her sassy cheeks again, and again, his teeth clenched and his eyes burning. Marion groaned, a mixture of pain and pleasure, her body trembling. Jerry noted her reaction and exulted, smacking her ass a rippling, reddening cheek at a time.

'God!' she gasped, rocking with the blows.

174

He grinned evilly, ecstatic to find that his in-control, sex-conventional girlfriend was enjoying his brutal expression of affection, was getting off on it as much as he was. 'I'm not hurting you, am I, my dear?' he hissed in her ear, spanking her bottom.

She shook her head, quick and tight. 'No-no, but… I've-I've got to get ready for work…'

'Work can wait!' he rasped.

He slapped her right cheek, her left, setting the brown, blushing flesh in motion again. She bowed her head down and pushed her butt back, shimmering brown hair falling over her face, fingernails clawing into the wood of the dresser.

Jerry's cock was a fire-forged rod of steel straining to part Marion's plush butt cheeks, jumping each and every time he smacked her bottom. He set his hand in a rigid, horizontal paddling position, bent his knees and spanked both of Marion's jiggling pillows at once.

The crack of his hand was loud, the shriek from her lips even louder. He smacked her over and over, the dresser creaking with the strain, the girl vibrating, wicked ass-flesh shuddering. Marion's bum had gone electric, the brutal, blessed impact of Jerry's flattened hand on her ass sending sexual sparks arcing all through her, setting her body to shimmering, her spank-sensitivity wildly out in the open.

'You like being spanked, don't you?' Jerry gritted rhetorically, one-handing her with abandon.

She nodded, shaking uncontrollably.

He ceased his butt-heating long enough to yank her thong down, fully exposing the crevice between her cheeks. She pressed her legs together and bent forward at the waist, presenting a clear and lush twin-mounded target for his pleasurably punishing hands. He fanned her rippling cheeks with an open palm, raining blow after blow down upon her, whaling her ass, waxing her bottom. She whimpered with joy, butt blazing fiery red under the onslaught.

175

When his hand was stinging too much for even him to stand, Jerry dropped to his knees and dug under the bed and extracted the foot-long leather strap he'd been saving for just such a special occasion. It was the kind of strap school principals used to use to discipline unruly children. He gazed at Marion's bright, impudent bum, tapping the stiffened leather against an open hand. Then he whacked the girl's bottom with it.

She moaned, rocking forward, twisting her head around to give her lover/punisher a shaky smile, her eyes gone watery. He strapped her perfect ass, the blows striking blistering white before being consumed by crimson. Sweat streamed down his face as tears streamed down hers, his raging hard-on swinging away with the strap.

He whipped Marion's outrageous bottom until she was teetering on the very brink of unconsciousness, her butt gone numb but not unfeeling, her cheeks brick-red and burning, ridges forming where the strap had fallen most harshly.

Finally, he dropped the ass-bashing device and dug into a drawer of the dresser, pulling out a bottle of lube. 'Ever been fucked up the ass?' he growled, oiling his angry erection.

She stared at him in the mirror, mascara streaking her cheeks, arms and legs trembling all on their own. 'N-no,' she gulped.

He slid his greasy fingers in between her ravaged cheeks, and she moaned. His forefinger sought out her opening, squirming all the way to the knuckle inside of her. Then he rotated the digit, and smacked her brilliant bum at the same time.

Marion cried out, as dizzy with lust as he was; the blood rushing to her pussy and ass, pounding in her ears. She peeled the fingers of her right hand off the dresser and sent them diving down to her pussy. She was inconsolably wet, and she desperately rubbed her clit, her body jumping and buzzing with Jerry's every hand fall and finger twist.

He eventually eased his digit out of her butthole, replaced it with his cockhead, his shiny, bloated hood pushing against the girl's tiny virgin opening. He gripped his pole and gritted his teeth and pressed forward, popping her anal cherry with a ruthlessness borne of basest necessity, his cockhead punching through her pucker and shoving inside her anus.

'Oh… God!' Marion breathed.

Jerry dug his fingers into her hot, sweat-dappled skin and relentlessly ploughed ahead, battering-ram cock boring inside her. He sank his spike into her split-peach bottom until balls kissed butt-flesh. 'Fuck, you're tight!' he grunted, buried to the hairline in Marion's swollen rear-end.

He started moving his hips, churning his cock back and forth in her gripping chute, the heat and vice-like tightness, the cock's eye view of the girl's tenderised bottom setting his balls to boiling. She rubbed her puffed-up clit faster and faster, her whole body quivering, the stuffed-full feeling of having a big, fat cock up her ass setting her head to spinning and her pussy to tingling.

'Fuck me! Fuck my ass!' she shrieked, buffing her clit with abandon.

Jerry pounded cock into her ass, smacking her brutalised derriere with his body now as he wildly thrust forward, the crack of hot, wet flesh coming together filling the humid bedroom. His balls suddenly tightened, and he ramped up the fucking even more, recklessly ramming her butt, her crimson cheeks shuddering non-stop. He was jolted by orgasm, blasting white-hot semen deep into Marion's ass.

'Yes!' she screamed, jerking with her own ecstasy, her hand a blur on her pussy.

He kept on plunging away, spraying sperm into her anus, her gushing exclamations of joy urging him on.

When it was finally all over, he collapsed over the top of her, their bodies glued together with their wicked exertion, his cock still plugged full-length into her ass. She buried her head in her arms and struggled to get her breath back. Then she remembered her job, and Jerry eased his still-hard member out of her raw, violated butthole and helped her dress.

The rounded bottoms of her butt cheeks peeked a ravaged scarlet out from beneath the hem of her frilly skirt.

'A few of the customers asked Tony, the bartender, if someone had been roughing me up – a jealous boyfriend or something.' Marion sat down gingerly on the edge of the bed and carefully rolled off a stocking.

Jerry grinned sleepily, stretched out contentedly on the bed. 'I bet your tips were even better than usual.'

'Maybe. But that's not the point, Jerry. You could have cost me my job.'

'Really?' he said, grinning some more.

Marion smiled shyly and slid her arms around his neck. Her eyes were warm and moist. She kissed him. 'It's-it's just that I'm kind of... sensitive down there.'

Jerry lightly squeezed her battered bottom. 'So I noticed.' He kissed her. 'You've got a million dollar booty, baby, and you like getting it worked over. And I just happen to be a buttman from way back. We were meant for each other.'

She bit her lip. 'I wonder if we, um, share another... fetish?'

He laughed, playfully squeezed her cheek again. 'Try me and find out.' He was a guy never averse to pumping up the kink.

And five minutes later, he was a 'guy' clad in a satiny pink bra and shiny pink panties, his hairy legs straining the snow-white fabric of Marion's best pair of stockings.

She smiled, eyes gleaming. 'Very fetching, darling.'

Jerry smiled back. He wasn't admitting it – yet – but cross-dressing was one of his favourite bedroom role-playing activities. He now knew for sure that this butt-blessed and blasted, open-minded girl was definitely a keeper.

Marion shimmied out of her French maid outfit and peeled away the thong, strolled over to her 'man' and roughly cupped his balls through the silky material of her panties. A shiver of delight raced up Jerry's spine, a lightning bolt streaked through Marion's pussy. 'A pretty girl like you needs some make-up to really bring out the inner-tart,' she said.

He eagerly nodded, and she pulled him over to the dresser and pushed him down into a chair, began liberally applying blush and lipstick and mascara and eye shadow to his unshaven face. And when he was all powdered and painted up like the slut he was, she fucked him in the ass with the strap-on dildo she'd picked up after work. The leather straps chafed her tender bottom, but she wasn't complaining.

And neither was Jerry.

Until the crack of dawn, that is, when he tried to clean himself up for the class of eager-beaver young women he taught at a local all-girls high school. He frantically scrubbed his face, but the indelible lipstick and eye shadow just wouldn't budge.

Marion smiled dreamily as her guy cried out in anguish, picturing him delivering a lecture to his nubile, starry-eyed students while done up like a whore. Revenge was sweet. Sweeter still, when she thought about the spanking she most certainly deserved and would get for being such a naughty girl.

# Customer Satisfaction
## by Elizabeth Coldwell

When he slipped into the shop just before closing time, I thought I recognised his little secret immediately. I had only been working in Belle's Boudoir for a couple of months, but that was more than long enough to recognise the furtive glances and nervous manner of the first-time customer.

I was preoccupied with making sure all the necessary checks were done to ensure I could lock up at the end of the day, without Belle worrying I was making a mess of running the shop in her absence. Otherwise I might have noticed that he was actually paying far too much attention to the cut and fabric of certain garments to be a novice in the world of lingerie.

Mentally, I had him down as someone shopping for a new girlfriend, looking for something which he would find sexy and she wouldn't find cheap. Not that we stocked cheap: there were no sleazy nylon crotchless panties or tacky scarlet-and-black cami and French knicker sets with scratchy lace round the leg holes. Those were strictly for the sex shops and downmarket online retailers. Belle's Boudoir was chic and classy, all silk, satin and designer brands. If you wanted something deliciously saucy such as a pearl-encrusted thong or teasing tie-sided stripper knickers, you would find it here. And I was sure we had more than enough choice to satisfy this particular customer.

Maybe I was biased, but I was thinking the best of him because he was cute. Six foot tall, easily, with spiky, blond-streaked hair and the stocky, muscular build of someone who played a lot of sport. He didn't strike me as the type who would ask for two sets of identical lingerie, one for his wife and another – usually two sizes smaller – for his mistress. Or eye me up and down and tell me he was shopping for a woman who was 'about my size', and could I help him by modelling this bra or that pair of knickers? This, I thought, was going to be a nice straightforward sale, the last of the day before I could lock up and go home.

He was looking at two pairs of silk panties now, one in a pretty shell pink and the other in subtle ivory, obviously trying to choose between them. I gave him a couple of moments, then walked over to where he was standing. 'Can I help you with those?' I asked.

He blushed slightly; it made him look even more boyish and appealing. 'It's difficult,' he said, 'they're both so beautiful…'

'We sell a lot of the ivory,' I told him. I took a subtle glance at his ring finger and noted the lack of a wedding band. 'It's a nice, safe choice, particularly for someone you don't know very well or haven't been seeing that long. But my favourites are the pink. Of course, you could always spoil her and buy both of them…'

This time the blush was more pronounced, the hesitation longer before he finally replied, 'Actually, I'm trying to decide on the colour because I'm buying them for myself.'

It took all my self-composure not to gape at him. It wasn't that I had never heard of a man wanting to wear women's underwear. Belle had told me often enough about some of her more specialised customers, and assured me that it would only be a matter of time before I served one of them myself. But the men she described or had even, on occasion, discreetly pointed out to me, were nothing like the one who stood before me now. They were, more often than

182

not, in their forties or older, and had carefully arched brows, soft, electrolysed skin without a hint of five o'clock shadow or hair which was long enough to look feminine with the aid of a little careful styling – all the hallmarks of the stereotypical cross-dresser. There was nothing feminine about my current customer – apart, it seemed, from his choice of undergarment. So much for stereotypes.

When I didn't laugh or ask him to leave the shop, he relaxed visibly. 'I – er – don't suppose I could try them on, could I?'

We had a couple of curtained-off cubicles at the back of the shop, which were mostly used for customers to try on trickier garments like corsets and basques, and where we also carried out bra fittings. I had no idea how Belle would have reacted to such a request, but the thought of this gorgeous man slipping into a pair of silk panties was one I was suddenly finding too arousing to resist. Particularly as I was now remembering something else Belle had explained to me – the concept of the panty slave, who liked a woman to order him around once he was wearing his knickers.

'Let me just lock the door first,' I said. 'It'll make sure you have all the privacy you need.'

He nodded, standing clutching his prospective purchases as though he couldn't bear to be parted from them. I turned the sign in the shop door to 'CLOSED' and then ushered him towards one of the cubicles.

He pulled the curtain shut behind him. I hovered discreetly outside, as I would with any other customer, trying not to listen too intently to the sound of a zip being unfastened and something heavy, like a belt buckle, clunking on the floor. As the seconds ticked past, I became aware that there was a pulse beating heavily in my crotch, a wetness trickling into my own panties as my imagination ran wild with thoughts of what might be happening behind that flimsy curtain. I was filled with the dark, powerful urge to slip a hand under my skirt and give my pussy the stroking it was beginning to crave.

I started guiltily as a blond head emerged from round the side of the curtain. 'I tried the pink ones, like you suggested,' he said. 'I was just wondering what you thought?'

The invitation was obvious, but if I stepped into the cubicle, I was in severe danger of doing something that would, if Belle ever found out about it, more than likely see me dismissed from my job. And then I decided that Belle would never find out – and that even if she did, I didn't care. I simply had to see for myself what he looked like in those panties.

The sight which greeted my eyes almost made me whimper with lust. He was wearing nothing but a white T-shirt which stretched tautly across his well-defined chest, and the panties. The thin silk was fighting a futile battle to contain his bulging cock, and his own excitement was evident by the spot of moisture which already dampened the fabric.

'Well, how do I look?' he asked.

I couldn't help replying, 'Surely you mean, "How do I look, mistress?"' If, as I hoped, he was dressing to bring out his inner slave, he would correct himself. He did. I felt a sudden, delicious rush of power, and my pussy twitched in triumphant anticipation.

'You look almost good enough to eat,' I told him.

His blue eyes widened. 'Only almost?'

'Losing the T-shirt would be an improvement,' I said, and watched as, in one casual movement, he pulled the garment over his head and tossed it to the floor. I smiled, eyeing his muscular torso. 'Better. Much, much better.'

I dropped to my knees before him. 'What are you doing – er, mistress?' he asked.

'I want to make sure of the fit.'

Gently, I ran my fingers across the front of his panties. His breathing quickened, and for a moment he gave into the sensations, then he seemed to recover himself and caught hold of my hand.

'I'm sorry,' I said. 'Have I gone too far? It's OK, we can stop the game now.'

He shook his head. 'No, I like it. It's just that I've never done anything like this. I mean, until a few days ago, no one else even knew about my fetish. I just used to borrow things out of the laundry basket and try them on. And I used to buy pairs for my ex-girlfriend specifically so I could wear them when she wasn't around. And then she came home early and caught me in the thong I bought her for Valentine's Day – and that's why she's my ex-girlfriend.'

So that was why he was out shopping for his own. 'Don't worry,' I told him. 'I'm a lot more understanding than she was. But you also know that you have to please a mistress who is so kind and understanding, don't you?'

He nodded, by now apparently more than willing to do anything I asked of him. His grip on my wrist was different, as he began to encourage me to caress him. That was a little forward, but I would let it go. I could always reprimand him later. As I played with him, I couldn't help but notice the sensuous contrast between the hardness of his cock and the softness of the panties, but as much fun as rubbing him might have been, I had other ideas.

I pulled my hand away sharply. 'Never forget your mistress' pleasure comes first,' I reminded him.

Obediently, he dropped to his knees. As I held my skirt up around my waist, he eased my panties carefully down, encouraging me to step out of them. He lifted the delicate fabric to his nose, reverently breathing in my aroma, spicier than it would have been after a normal day in the boutique thanks to the events of the last few minutes.

He looked up at me with lust and what could have been adoration in his eyes. I knew I must have looked good, with

185

my trimmed pussy framed by the lacy straps of my suspenders, but I suspected he was also appreciating the fact I not only understood his need to wear panties, I was getting just as much pleasure from it as he was.

More in fact, when I felt the tip of his tongue press against my sex lips, seeking out and finding my clit. I widened my stance, giving him easier access to all my hidden places. He quickly learned where I liked the soft pressure of his tongue best, guided by my little gasps and murmurs of encouragement, and as he lapped away I found myself thinking how stupid his ex-girlfriend had been to let his love for panties scare her off. To have a man worshipping you with his mouth was the finest of pleasures, I thought, as he gave my pussy the last few, quick licks it took to send me spiralling up into my climax.

I hugged his head to me until my knees finally stopped trembling, and then I let him go. He gazed at me, his chin glazed with my juices, and I smiled. 'Beautifully done, slave,' I told him. 'And now it's time for your reward.'

I bent and dropped a little kiss on the end of his cock where it was staining the fabric with his arousal, then began to mouth him in earnest through the panties. With one hand, I held on to his firm thigh, which was covered in fuzzy blond hair. If he'd been a dedicated transvestite, instead of just a man who loved the feel of women's undies, those thighs would have been shaven smooth and not half as much fun to fondle.

I felt his hands tangling in my hair, encouraging the movements of my rapidly bobbing head. He was so excited now that the head of his cock had poked free of the panties, and I took it deeper in my mouth, savouring the taste and smell of him. The wet suction of my lips around his shaft was bringing him ever closer to orgasm, but it was when I whispered, 'That's it, come for me, slave,' that he groaned and released his come. I drew back from him, letting the pearly strings dribble out of the side of my mouth.

He lifted me to my feet, clasping me to his bare chest. 'Thank you,' he said, and kissed the top of my head.

'So you've decided on the pink, then?' I asked him, as he began to reach for his scattered clothes.

He paused in the act of pulling his T-shirt back on, and flashed me a wicked smile. 'Well, I was thinking of treating myself to the pink *and* the white. But if you're working tomorrow afternoon, I thought I might come back then. There's a pair with a rosebud print I quite fancy trying on...'

# Let The Punishment Fit The Crime
## by Chloe Devlin

Huish! Huish! That's the whippy sound of the cane I hear as my Master swishes it back and forth next to my ear. I also know the sound it makes as it strikes my flesh. Thwack! Thwack!

But that's not what I hear right now. And definitely not what I feel. For my Master has devised another sort of punishment for me this evening. Instead of the glorious freedom in receiving the smacks of his hand, the paddle or whatever implement he chooses to use to warm my flesh, he's chosen to deny me the exquisite sensations of being punished by his hand.

Instead, I'm being forced to listen to him punish another. I'm not allowed to witness the act or even be in the same room when he punishes her.

But listen to them, I must.

'Are you comfortable, pet?' he asks.

Comfortable? How do I answer that? I suppose the plush of the velour that covers the recliner is comfortable against my bare skin. So my back and butt are comfortable. But I wouldn't exactly call the ropes that twine about my waist and bisect the lips of my cunt comfortable. Abrasive? A bit. Tightly tied? Of course. Arousing? Yes!

But not comfortable.

I know my expressions are flitting across my face. It's something I just can't control no matter how hard I try. So my Master divines that my answer is conflicted.

'Let me rephrase that, pet,' he says as he touches the tip of the cane to the inside of my right thigh. 'Do you wish to be untied?'

'Oh, no, Master!' The words gush out before I can stop them. 'I'm ready for whatever you desire.'

He traces a line up the inside of my thigh until he reaches my knee, then continues back down the inside of the other thigh. The tiny imperfections in the bamboo catch and scrape my delicate flesh. I bite my lip to keep from moaning out loud when he stops and removes the cane. 'Very well, pet. It's time for me to begin.'

'Yes, Master.'

His fingers grip my chin, holding me steady. I can feel the warmth of his breath inches from my lips. 'Remember – this is your punishment. If you'd listened carefully to me, you could be the one enjoying my attentions. Instead you will listen to every sound I make as I strike Melody's body. Her body instead of yours.'

Miserable because I know it could've been me receiving the wonder of my Master's punishment, I say the only thing I can. 'Yes, Master.'

A hard kiss covers my lips, his tongue ravaging my mouth before leaving me gasping for air. Then all that's left for me is to wait. And my position isn't really all that uncomfortable.

After all, I'm not hanging by my wrists or bent backwards over a barrel. Instead, I'm sitting in a brown velour recliner. My legs are apart and my ankles are tied to the armrests, leaving me spread wide open. Although my arms are buckled above my head, they're not pulled in an awkward pose or stretched unbearably tight – just above my head so they're out of the way.

My Master also took a rope, twined it around my waist, then down through my crotch, leaving my pussy lips on either side. Coming up at the back, the rope slides between my butt cheeks, resting against my asshole before being tied off on the line around my waist.

But despite the fact that this is supposed to be my punishment, my Master was kind enough to attach a set of nipple clamps to my hard buds, leaving a chain hanging from them.

And of course, being blindfolded I can't see any of this. Once everything had been attached to his satisfaction, my Master slipped a black silk scarf over my eyes, tying it so I can't see anything.

Slap! Slap! Slap! Slap! I jump as though I've been spanked. But these are just the sounds of Master's hand on Melody's butt. I wish it was my ass that was receiving them.

I know just how they feel. Slap! Slap! With his hand cupped, the sound of Master's spanking is worse than the burn. But it still smarts every time his hand comes down.

The clamps on my nipples grow tighter as my buds become even harder and more sensitive. The tingling in my tits is a tease for all the other lovely sensations I could be enjoying – if only I were the one being punished. Instead of cool air wafting against my bare pussy, the rasp of the cane would rub against my engorged clit. If I was performing exceptionally well, I might even receive the gift of Master's thumb in my anus.

Slap! Slap! Melody grunts at a particularly hard strike. But she hasn't cried out yet. I wonder if the paddle or the cane will force a sound from her. Finally the slaps stop, all I hear is Melody's panting combined with my Master's harsh breathing. Then a steady swish-swish sound overlays everything. I strain to identify it. I know it's not the paddle or cane – those would make sharper noises as they hit

Melody's skin. This is a softer noise, almost like skin rubbing against skin.

I listen for a few more seconds before it comes to me. It's the suede flogger that Master uses on my tits.

I wonder if Melody's enjoying it. Does she feel that same tingling in her breasts, the same streaks of excitement flowing from her tits to her clit? Soft whimpers of delight fill the air and I know she's loving every minute of her punishment.

Wetness seeps from my slit and soaks the rope that presses against my pussy. I wriggle my hips, trying to get some sort of friction against my swollen clit. But all I manage to do is increase my excitement, without satisfying myself at all.

The soft swish-swish of the suede flogger continues without letting up. I can almost imagine the motion that my Master's wrist makes in order to keep the suede strands gently rubbing against Melody's body. Her nipples must be nearly as hard and tight as mine. Master won't attach clamps to hers as long as he's flogging them. But afterward…

Afterward, he'll delicately pinch, then attach them to each hardened bud before continuing with her punishment.

Silence greets my straining ears. No more swish-swish, no more whimpers, not even heavy breathing. I wish I knew what was going on. All I can do is listen and imagine. But without sounds, I have no idea.

Breaking the silence of the darkness, my Master says, 'You're doing wonderfully, Melody. Now, it's time for the paddle. Nod if you're ready.' A pause. 'Splendid. Now, remember, don't tense up and it won't hurt as much.'

How can he be so nice to her? She's just a tool he's using to punish me. But he's even using her real name. Whack! The first strike of the paddle cuts into my envious thoughts. I wish it was my ass that was receiving the hits.

Whack! But my Master has chosen the perfect punishment. He withholds the slaps and whacks that I crave, while making me listen as he gives them to another. After this is over, I'll never misbehave like that again.

Whack! I knew better than to try and manipulate my Master into spanking me. He's the one in charge and I'm the one who obeys. But I thought I was smarter and could get him to give me the spanking my butt was craving. Instead, here I am, tied to the recliner, my legs spread wide with a rope exciting my pussy and clamps arousing my nipples, listening to my beloved Master giving *my* punishment to another.

Several more whacks echo in my ears, combined with grunts from Melody. I know she's enjoying the beating and that arouses me even more, despite my jealousy.

Then the most exciting sound reaches my ears. Huish-huish. I know that sound. Master is flicking the cane back and forth against the air.

Huish thwack! Immediately after the strike, a cry fills my ears. Melody has finally broken. But even her cry contains her ecstasy. It's that indefinable sensation that's part pain and part pleasure. And you can't decide which you want more. The cry is familiar to me since it's one that I make when Master canes me. But now, I can only listen and wish it was me.

Huish thwack! Huish thwack! I wiggle my ass against the velour, wanted to feel the sting of the cane instead of the softness of the plush fabric.

I count out three more strikes of the cane then Melody lets out a soft sigh. Maybe Master is running his palm over her burning flesh. When her sigh turns to a hiss, I know that he's reached the raised stripes made by the cane. Those marks should be on my skin, not hers.

Panting breaths move into the room, closer to where I'm sitting. What is Master going to do now? He's already used his hand, the suede flogger, the paddle and the cane. What's next?

'Over the back of the sofa, Melody,' he says. 'And keep your legs spread.'

My eyes widen underneath the black blindfold. He's going to fuck her. I just know it. He's bending her over the back of the sofa so her pussy will be at just the right height. Then he's going to fuck her.

Oh, he's devised a truly devious punishment for me. Not only have I been forced to listen to him punish another, but now I have to listen to him fuck her, too.

I catch a whiff of his cologne and his voice whispers in my ear. 'Just think, pet. This could've been you. I want you to remember that. I could be preparing to fuck you instead of Melody.'

Before I can respond, he moves away. I know this because I lose his spicy scent and the warmth of his breath against my ear. I draw in a deep breath, trying to keep from begging Master to fuck me instead. I know he won't. Once his mind is made up, it takes a lot to change it. Certainly more than a bit of begging and pleading from me.

'Stand still, Melody,' Master says. 'I'm going deeper.'

His hips slap against her buttocks. I hear the squishy wetness as his cock plunges into her wet pussy. But I'm sure that her cunt isn't as sopping as mine. I've been dripping pussy juice so much it's like I'm sitting in a puddle.

'So hot, so tight,' Master hisses. 'That's it, squeeze tighter.'

My inner muscles clench in response to his order, wishing his cock was inside me. I could hold him tighter than she could. But instead, all I feel is air. The rope rubs against my clit. A little harder and I might even be able to come. But my legs are tied too tightly and I can only shift back and forth a little bit.

'That's it, Melody. Hold it right there. I'm going to come!' Master's voice rises with his passion.

I bite my lip to keep from crying out and begging Master to fuck me, too. To let me come. His fingers, his cock, I don't care. I just want to come.

'Take it, Melody' he growls. 'That's it, take my come!'

I listen to each groan, imagining the spasms of pleasure shuddering through his body. I can practically feel his fluid flooding my body as he spurts inside me.

But it's not my body he's coming in, it's Melody's. The punishment has been more than effective. I know that I'll never disobey him. I'll never try to manipulate him into spanking me, or fucking me or anything else. I'll be the perfect little pet, ready for anything he wishes.

His hand caresses my cheek and I nuzzle into his palm, trying to show him how sorry I am without speaking. 'Have you learned your lesson, pet?'

I nod, the calluses on his palm gently rasping against the corner of my mouth, my lips tingling. 'Yes, Master.'

'You've taken your punishment well so far, pet,' he says. 'To make sure the lesson stays with you, I'm going to have Melody suck me off while you watch. I'll remove your blindfold, but nothing else. The final bit of punishment is no orgasms for you today. At all.'

'Yes, Master,' I whisper. 'Thank you, Master.'

As my Master removes the black silk blindfold, I blink against the subdued lights of the living room, having been in the dark for so long. Then I turn my head, like a good pet, to watch as my Master gets his cock sucked.

Tomorrow, it will be my turn.

# Imagine great sex on your doormat every month!

- Imagine a new Xcite book landing on your door mat every month.
- Imagine reading the twenty varied and exciting stories that each book contains.
- Imagine that three books are absolutely FREE as is the postage and packing.

**No hassles**
**No shopping**
**Just pure fun**

Yes! that's the Xcite subscription deal –
for just £69.99 (a saving of over £25) you will get 12 books
with free P&P delivered by Royal Mail (UK addresses only)

All books are discreetly and perfectly packaged
Credit cards are billed to Accent Press ltd

Order now at www.xcitebooks.com
or call 01443 710930

*Play together!*

**'If, as a couple, you have not watched an erotic film together
this would be a perfect opportunity to dip your toe gently in.'**

Scarlet Magazine

## Erotic Films on demand

**Watch now by logging onto:**

# www.joybear.com

*Special Online Offer for Xcite Readers!*

All our films online are split into scenes, giving you greater choice and DVD quality. We
are delighted to present Xcite readers with a special buy one get one free offer. Simply
choose any two scenes and we will only charge you for one. Please enter the promo-
tional code below when prompted:

XCITEJOY01

199

# Also available from Xcite Books:
## (www.xcitebooks.com)

| | | |
|---|---|---|
| **Sex & Seduction** | **1905170785** | **price £7.99** |
| **Sex & Satisfaction** | **1905170777** | **price £7.99** |
| **Sex & Submission** | **1905170793** | **price £7.99** |
| | | |
| **5 Minute Fantasies 1** | **1905170610** | **price £7.99** |
| **5 Minute Fantasies 2** | **190517070X** | **price £7.99** |
| **5 Minute Fantasies 3** | **1905170718** | **price £7.99** |
| | | |
| **Whip Me** | **1905170920** | **price £7.99** |
| **Spank Me** | **1905170939** | **price £7.99** |
| **Tie Me Up** | **1905170947** | **price £7.99** |
| | | |
| **Ultimate Sins** | **1905170599** | **price £7.99** |
| **Ultimate Sex** | **1905170955** | **price £7.99** |
| **Ultimate Submission** | **1905170963** | **price £7.99** |